ELLIE'S WAR
Wherever You Are

EMILY SHARRATT

SCHOLASTIC

Scholastic Children's Books
An imprint of Scholastic Ltd
Euston House, 24 Eversholt Street, London, NW1 1DB, UK
Registered office: Westfield Road, Southam, Warwickshire, CV47 0RA
SCHOLASTIC and associated logos are trademarks and/or
registered trademarks of Scholastic Inc.

First published in the UK by Scholastic Ltd, 2015

Text copyright © Scholastic Ltd, 2015

ISBN 978 1407 14497 9

A CIP catalogue record for this book
is available from the British Library.

Printed by CPI Group (UK) Ltd, Croydon, CR0 4YY
Papers used by Scholastic Children's Books are made
from wood grown in sustainable forests.

1 3 5 7 9 10 8 6 4 2

This is
and dialo
fictitio

Huge thanks to Emma Young

One

August 1915

The oak tree stood proud in the heart of the wood. It was older than the village of Endstone, older than all the other trees around it. Although it was late summer, the tree was still lush and green, its upper branches reaching out to create a shaded canopy over the woodland floor, the lower ones bowing deep to offer a convenient scaffold for climbing, which Ellie Phillips and her best friend, Jack Scott, had relished over the years.

Ellie looked up at the branches and could hardly remember the little girl she had been – hair tangled with leaves, cheeks pink with excitement. The memories seemed sun-bleached and faded, well-worn and somehow unreal, as though she had read about them in one of her favourite books.

The wood was hushed apart from the sound of birdsong, a gentle breeze whistling through the branches and causing them to creak, the splashing of the river and the furtive scamperings and scuffles of small creatures foraging amongst the leaves and acorns.

But as Ellie stood perfectly still, clasping a lumpy pair of red woollen gloves to her chest, she almost thought she could make out the voices of children:

"Not that branch, El. It won't take your weight."

"Speak for yourself, lardy. Just watch me."

"Well, don't come crying to me if you fall and break every bone in your body."

And then another voice from the ground below, a man's:

"Oh, please don't. Your mother would have my

guts for garters."

"El."

Ellie startled as her friend's voice scattered her imaginings.

"Are you ready?"

Jack stood beside her, leaning on a shovel. She wasn't the only one who had changed, Ellie thought to herself. Jack was almost six foot now, broad and strong from hours of physical work at the factory. The freckles covering his face and arms were the same as ever though. So was the tousled brown hair, the smooth, pink-splashed cheeks and the blue eyes fringed with surprisingly dark lashes.

As she stared at him, he cocked his head quizzically and his mouth quirked into that familiar crooked grin. Another thing that hadn't changed.

"El?" he repeated.

"Sorry, yes." She screwed her eyes tight for a second. "Yes, I'm ready."

"Come on, then." He reached out and took her hand, leading her gently towards the small hole he had dug at the base of the tree.

Dropping to her knees, Ellie placed the woollen gloves in the hole and sat for a moment, resting her hand on them. Closing her eyes again, she pictured her father sitting in just this spot, medical journals spread out beside him, eyebrows creased in concentration, pencil gripped between his lips. She remembered how his face would brighten when he saw her coming. He would shake the books from his lap, spring to his feet and gather her in a bear hug.

Jack crouched beside her and together they swept the soil back into the hole and smoothed it over. Jack pressed a pretty white shell on top. When they had finished, he took her hand again, and she drew a deep breath.

"Sleep well, Daddy," she began in a steady voice. "You are the best person I've ever known. I miss you every day, and I will love you for ever." A tear splashed down her cheek and she felt more gathering in its wake.

Jack pulled her into his chest and wrapped his arms around her, resting his chin on her head. Her tears didn't fall, but her ribs felt tight, as though her lungs were trying to burst out. Her brain felt swollen inside her skull and her hair tugged painfully on her scalp. She pulled away from Jack's arms, noticing that his eyes were glistening too, his jaw clamped.

"Do you think he ever got to wear them?" she asked.

He wiped his nose roughly with the back of his hand. "Eh?"

"Father. The gloves. They can barely have arrived before..."

"Oh." He took a moment before trusting himself to speak. "I'm sure he did, El. They were with his other things that were returned to you, weren't they?"

Ellie nodded.

"So he'd obviously received them. If I know your dad, he'll have put them straight on to show to the other lads." Jack put on her father's hearty public-school voice, so accurate it made Ellie's chest contract. "'What did I tell you, boys? My daughter's the cleverest girl in Endstone, and the prettiest, but she can't knit for toffee!'"

Ellie gave a snorting laugh that turned into a sob midway, and slumped back against her friend. She pressed her handkerchief to her eyes, until Jack seized it to blow his own nose, making the pair of them laugh and cry all over again.

"Was I mean not to bring Mother and Charlie?" she asked, after a few moments' silence.

"No," Jack replied firmly. "You were right. The service Reverend Chester held back when we first heard the news was more your mam's kind of thing. She wouldn't have understood this."

"I know, I know. It's just…" She reclaimed the now-soggy handkerchief. "Ugh, Jack… It's just… I'm sure Father would have wanted us to be together when we said … goodbye … to him."

Jack used a grubby thumb to catch the errant tear as it tumbled from her lashes. "El, when this is all over, you and your mam and Charlie can go to France, to where he's buried, and you can say goodbye to him together then."

Ellie closed her eyes against the thought of that hastily dug grave, of Father alone and so far from home. No, not alone, she supposed, there would be thousands of his comrades there too. "Maybe," was all she said. She couldn't imagine her mother ever making such a trip. But *she* would do it, she decided, and she would take a shell just like the one they'd put in the earth here; a little piece of Endstone to remain with her father in France.

"Come on, little mother," Jack said, standing and hauling her to her feet beside him. "We'd best be getting you home."

"Don't call me that!" Ellie said crossly, her expression darkening.

It was the last day of the summer holidays. Tomorrow she should have been returning to school. But a week ago, to her great surprise, her mother had announced that she would be going to work in the factory. Previously the factory had made furnaces for marine engines, but recently it had begun to produce munitions. Her mother's new job meant Ellie would have to stay at home to look after her little brother, Charlie.

"Sorry." Jack grinned sheepishly. "But, El, you've always hated school. You've been wanting to get out of that place for ever."

"I know! But not so I could stay at home and be a housewife! I love Charlie, and I don't mind helping out – of course I don't – but how am I ever supposed to do anything with my life if I'm stuck at home?

Father would never have allowed this! My education cut sh—"

"El," Jack shushed her, "get down from your soapbox. You don't have to convince me! I'm on your side, remember?"

Ellie grunted as she clambered across the stile.

"Besides," Jack continued, as he hopped down next to her, "I don't mean any offence, but I can't imagine your mam lasting five minutes in that place! I've been there for years and even I'm finding it tougher than ever. It's not that parts for shells and bombs are any harder to make than ship engines, but they've got us doing longer hours than before, and we're expected to produce twice as much."

This was true. It was harder than ever to spend time with Jack. When he wasn't at work, he would be at home sleeping off his exhaustion.

"Then again, it's mostly women there these days, and they seem to be coping well enough. Great workers actually, lots of them."

Ellie rolled her eyes. "Why on earth wouldn't they be?"

"Oh, all right, Mrs Pankhurst, don't start on me.

I just mean, it's impressive – it's all new to them, isn't it?"

"I suppose so."

"But, I'll tell you what, they're all a lot hardier than your mam."

Ellie pictured her mother; her sharp, prominent bones, her pale, porcelain-delicate skin, her pursed lips. She thought of her almost-constant headaches, her nervous temperament and her tendency to take to her bed for the slightest reason.

"I've tried to tell her," she said at last. She didn't understand what had prompted this sudden decision of Mother's. "I mean, I know how it feels to want to *do* something, to—" She broke off at the sound of an engine, droning and unfamiliar. "Wait, Jack, look! What's that?"

They had reached the far corner of the village square, looking towards the sea. There, high in the sky, hovering above the distant waves, was a large dark blob, long and thin, with a rounded nose. It looked a bit like an enormous, flying fish, Ellie thought.

"It's a Zeppelin," Jack breathed.

Ellie gasped. She had read about the German

airships in the newspapers, but she would have been less surprised to see Buckingham Palace appear in the middle of the square than she was by the sight of this foreign craft hovering over her tiny village. "But . . . but what's it doing over here? What should we do?"

Others were gathering in the square, frozen by this alien vision. Arms were extended and cries of exclamation filled the air.

"Oh, it's too far away to be any danger to us." Jack's tones were filled with wonder. "No, it must be on its way to London."

"Poor London."

"Yes. . . Beautiful, though, isn't it?"

Following the crowd, they drifted across the square and towards the seashore, their eyes still fixed on the Zeppelin.

"I don't know about beautiful. . ." Ellie said doubtfully.

They scuffed their feet along the pebbles of Big Beach, watching the ship as it drew closer to shore, following the trajectory of the slowly sinking sun. The growling sound, though still distant, was growing louder.

10

"Looks as though the war might arrive over here before I can get to France," Jack said. His chin was pointing straight up at the sky; he was leaning back so far he looked like he might topple over.

Ellie laughed, putting her hand behind his back to prop him up. "Well, it already has in a way. Look at the Mertens. Apparently, thousands and thousands of Belgian refugees have arrived in Folkestone this year already. More will end up here in Endstone, I'm sure."

The Mertens had arrived in January – a family of five fleeing the war in Belgium. The father, Julien, was a doctor and had been helping out in Ellie's father's old surgery, so the family had been given a house nearby, behind the main village square.

"True," said Jack. "It's a good thing they're here too. Poor old Thomas looked like he was going to collapse, trying to cope alone in the surgery. Especially with all the lads coming home injured."

"Well, maybe, but Dr Mertens will never replace Father."

"Of course not," Jack said, slinging an arm around her shoulders. "How could he? Listen,

El, try not to worry about staying home with old Charlie boy. You're tough. You'll be all right."

"I suppose I'll have to be."

She wished she could believe herself.

Two

Ellie pushed open the door to the village hall, her eyes taking a moment to adjust to the gloom after the soft, buttery light of the late summer's evening.

Her mother was sitting in a circle with twelve other women in the far corner of the room. The sun was streaming through the window on to their knitting. None of them looked up as she entered, absorbed in their murmured conversation and clacking needles.

Ellie watched her mother. She had always been slim, but now she was looking thin – gaunt, even. Ellie knew she wasn't eating enough; she tried to encourage her to have more at mealtimes but it was a struggle on top of coaxing Charlie to eat properly. There were deep grooves under her mother's eyes, furrows in her skin

13

that had been perfectly smooth not so long ago. Her skin had a greyish hue. Yet again, Ellie wondered how her mother would cope among the sturdier men and women at the factory.

On the other hand, she seemed to be in relatively high spirits. She wasn't smiling, quite, but she was speaking to Mrs Bramley with a degree of animation that Ellie didn't often see. Mrs Bramley's husband had also recently been killed in France. Their heads were bowed together as their fingers twined the wool over and around the needles. It was nice to see Mother getting along with one of the villagers for a change.

"Ellie!" came a shrill cry. Her little brother's solid form cannoned into her legs.

"*Oof!* Hello, Charlie," she said, taking his podgy hand and waving to the ladies of the knitting circle, who were all now looking her way.

"Good evening, Ellie," said Mrs Anderson with a smile. Her nine-month-old baby was rolling happily on a blanket at her feet, cooing to himself. Her husband was missing, presumed dead. He had met little Arthur for the first time when home on leave at Christmas.

"Good evening," Ellie replied, then offered greetings

to the other ladies in turn, before finally arriving in front of her mother.

"Hello, Eleanor," Josephine said. She was not smiling. "I do wish for once you could have managed to be on time."

"I am—" Ellie began to protest.

"You are not." Josephine cut across her crisply, causing several of the women to exchange glances. "I told you to collect Charlie at half past six, it is now twenty to seven. Kindly do not argue with me, Eleanor, just take Charlie home and get him ready for bed as I asked."

Ellie stood for a moment, feeling her nostrils flare. She took a couple of deep breaths to calm herself. Mrs Bramley gave her a small, sympathetic smile. Ellie puffed out a sigh, said, "Yes, Mother," and bid the others goodnight.

She fetched Charlie's pram from the porch, hefted him into it and began the journey home, bumping over the cobblestones. When they reached the edge of the square she had to bend almost at a right angle to power the pram up the steep hill to their cottage.

"Goodness, Charlie," she huffed, "you're getting

too heavy for this. You're going to have to walk by yourself soon, young man."

Charlie rubbed sleepily at his eyes with a grubby fist, but made no reply.

Ellie was out of breath and damp with sweat by the time they made it to the cottage. Glancing at the wisteria that climbed around the front door, she realized that it would need cutting back again soon or they wouldn't be able to get into the house.

Once inside, Ellie lifted Charlie from the pram and sat him at the table. She fetched butter and jam from the pantry and began to slice bread for his supper.

While her brother crammed sticky fistfuls into his mouth, Ellie lit a fire in the sitting room, set the metal tub before it and filled it with a mixture of cold water from the tap and hot from the kettle. The muscles in her back and shoulders felt tight and she reached her arms up to the ceiling to stretch them out.

Returning to the kitchen, she glanced out of the front window. Her mind wandered back to that day in January when she had glimpsed Mr Berry, Endstone's postman, coming up the path with the news from France.

16

They had been preparing vegetables for lunch. She remembered how her mother's expression had changed; the irritation at his knocking on the door draining away at the sight of the buff-coloured envelope he was clutching in his trembling hand.

Ellie shook her head, trying to shake off the memory.

She scooped Charlie down from his chair and ushered him into the living room. But as she peeled off his jam-smeared clothes and lifted him into the tub, her mind returned to the words of that awful letter.

It is my painful duty ... report received ...
notifying of the death of...

A tear dropped off the end of Ellie's chin, splashing into the bath water, followed by another then another. She'd been unable to cry for weeks and weeks after the letter, and the second one that had followed a few days' later from her father's platoon captain. Today it felt as though she would never stop.

She lathered soap through Charlie's blonde curls, shaping them into little horns to make him laugh. The captain's letter had offered sympathy and told them that he had been considered "one of the best in the company, the most trustworthy and respected", that he would be "greatly missed". The letter had also reassured them that death had been "instantaneous, and he could have felt no pain". Josephine had seemed to take some comfort from that – Ellie had heard her speaking to Reverend Chester of her gratitude for this "small mercy".

Ellie herself had been annoyed by the lack of detail in the letter. The platoon captain clearly hadn't known Father, not really. It sounded as though he were following a template. But she knew he wrote letters of this kind so often. It would be impossible to make them all truly personal.

For weeks Ellie had found herself going over and over her father's death in her mind, wondering how he had died, what he had thought about in his last moments, whether he had known he was dying. No matter how often she told herself that such thoughts were morbid, she just couldn't stop. Even now, eight months later, she would catch herself returning to these questions.

Charlie thumped his fist into the water, splashing suds at her face and reminding her of where she was. She fetched the towel, draped over the fireguard to warm, and bundled him up in it. Then she toiled up the stairs, his squirming body wet and heavy in her arms.

It must have been this afternoon's little memorial that had got her thinking this way again, she reflected as she towelled Charlie's hair dry. She went back in her mind to the first Sunday service after they had heard the news. It had seemed to Ellie as though Reverend Chester were talking about a stranger. It had felt unreal, disconnected from them, from her beloved father. Mother had scarcely raised her head for the whole service, but Ellie had been acutely aware of the stares of the fellow villagers – attention that was unwelcome, however well-meant.

She pulled Charlie's night-gown over his head and combed his hair. Each time she entered the church now, she felt the loss of her father anew. She dreaded the Sunday service. She knew that others found comfort in gathering together as a community, but Ellie's heart ached each time she listened to Reverend Chester insisting that the war was right, that their men had died with honour and glory... How could anything that brought such sadness to all their lives possibly be good?

She finished brushing Charlie's teeth and lifted him on to the little bed that he had slept in ever since outgrowing his cot. Already his curls were springing back into rebellious life. Normally she would read to him from one of his books of nursery rhymes but tonight she could see that his eyelids were heavy. Instead, she sat next to him, smoothing his hair until he fell asleep.

She dropped a kiss on to his forehead and pulled the thin summer blanket up to his chin. Moving over to her wardrobe, she rummaged around until, tucked away at the back, she found the small wooden box which contained all her most precious things.

A few weeks after his death, they had received a package containing her father's personal effects, including the gloves she had knitted him, and his wedding ring, which Ellie knew her mother now kept in her jewellery box. The package had also included a letter he had started but not finished, which talked about how they had spent Christmas on the front, and thanked his family for the parcel of treats they had sent, which he had shared with his fellow men.

She wasn't sure why she had kept the letter hidden away since she and her mother had first read it in January. She wished it was something she could share with her, but her father's death had made the distance between them feel wider than ever.

She lifted the letter from under the painted shell that Jack had given her last Christmas. Seeing her father's familiar handwriting, seeing the point at which he had broken off writing, presumably called away to do something else, made Ellie's eyes burn. The paper became fuzzy. She held it to her nose, but it smelled only of mothballs.

Even eight months after his death – a year since she had last seen him – a part of her still expected to hear his voice booming from downstairs, to see his face peek around the doorframe, come to kiss Charlie goodnight.

She wondered if that feeling would ever go away.

Three

The bell jangled as Ellie reversed out through the door of the village shop, pulling the pram with her. She called goodbye to Mrs Scott, Jack's mother, who ran the shop, helped by his sister, Anna, and set off across the square.

A stream of local children crossed her path and, with a jolt, she realized they were heading for school. It was the first day back. It felt strange not to be among them. Ellie had only ever missed school when she was unwell, or, last year, when she had to take care of Charlie and her mother when they were sick.

Two girls just a couple of years younger than Ellie were moving slowly at the back of the group, clearly in no hurry to get to school. They didn't even look her way. She wanted to shout after them, tell them how lucky they were. But why would they listen? She never had.

Putting her weight behind the pram, she began to push it back up the lane towards the cottage. Mother had left in the early hours, walking down to the station to catch the train with the other factory workers from the village. It was still dark when she had gone. Ellie had got up make her a cup of tea and see her off. Watching her walk down the hill in her worn, but still smart, grey jacket, Ellie wondered what her father would have thought at his wife, so beautiful and aloof, going off to do manual work. He wouldn't have been able to believe it, Ellie thought. She could scarcely believe it herself.

As usual Josephine had refused to give her daughter an explanation of any kind. She had simply announced that she wanted to do more for the war effort than just knitting. Ellie's fate had been decided without discussion.

Ellie and Charlie arrived home and went straight into the garden. Ellie picked the last of the peas, while Charlie chased the butterflies. His happy squeals made her smile but she kept a sharp eye on his proximity to the mud; the last thing she needed was to have to give him another bath.

"Knock, knock," a voice said cheerily. Thomas Pritchard appeared around the side of the house. The young doctor looked flustered and tired. He'd been working with Ellie's father before the war and had now taken over running the surgery – he was exempt from conscription on account of his limp. "I was knocking at the front, but I thought I could hear voices back here."

"Hello, Thomas," Ellie said, laying down her basket and brushing her hands clean against her apron. "Would you like a cup of tea and a piece of rhubarb pie? I made it yesterday."

"Thank you, Ellie, that sounds wonderful, but, no, I'm not stopping. Things are rather hectic at the surgery." He looked at her carefully. "I understand you won't be going to school any more."

Ellie felt her cheeks flare as she nodded.

"Well, I wondered if you might be able to help out at the surgery today. I've a day full of home visits ... the latest batch of wounded soldiers to be returned to us."

"What about Dr Mertens? I thought he was helping out now." Ellie was surprised to hear a note of bitterness in her voice and hoped that Thomas hadn't noticed it.

"He is, he is; he's been a godsend. But he's still finding his feet. And his English isn't quite perfect; it's making things harder for him in terms of reading, though you'd never know it to speak to him. It's not a problem when I'm around to help explain but when he's on his own..."

"I'm sorry," interrupted Ellie swiftly, "but I can't help. I have lots to do around here and I'm supposed to be minding Charlie."

"Oh, but Mrs Mertens loves children! I'm sure she'd be only too happy to look after young Ch—"

"She's a complete stranger to us!" Ellie cut across him. The doctor's mouth snapped shut. "I'm not leaving Charlie with someone we don't know; someone who doesn't even speak proper English!"

"I ... I understand. I'm sorry. I'll leave you to it." Thomas ruffled Charlie's hair. He smiled but his face betrayed his confusion, and he hurried away down the path at the side of the house.

Ellie returned to the peas with renewed vigour, hacking away at them savagely and pausing only to dash the back of her hand against her eyes. Suddenly she felt ashamed of her brusqueness with Thomas. The young doctor's kindness had been a constant, particularly in the months following her father's death. He was practically part of the family.

Where had this sudden anger come from?

Jack arrived later that afternoon, his fiddle in hand. His arrival was just in time; Ellie was on the verge of shouting at Charlie, who wouldn't get out from under her feet as she tried to make his tea. Jack played a frenzied, energetic tune that distracted Charlie and made him laugh, then switched to a soothing, slower piece to calm him down.

When Charlie was settled, the three of them sat at the table to eat the leek and potato soup Ellie had made. Ellie told Jack about her conversation with Thomas.

He watched her as she spoke. "Poor Thomas," he said, his mouth turning up at one corner. "*I* don't like to get on the wrong side of you and I'm a less delicate soul than he is!"

Ellie scowled but had to admit he was right. "It's not his fault..."

"What isn't?"

"Oh, I don't know. That I'm stuck at home with Charlie, I suppose. That I'm stuck here in Endstone, doing nothing of any use. That Father isn't coming back."

Jack patted her hand. "I know it feels strange still, but I really think it's a good job that Dr Mertens has come along. Poor Thomas was struggling to cope. He's not that much older than us, really. The new fellow has more experience and that's needed now."

"Hmm."

"And maybe you *should* see if his wife will mind Charlie for a bit. You always liked helping out at the surgery before."

"Well, I don't want to now, all right?" Ellie slammed down her soup spoon. "How could I bear to be there, seeing that man marching around my father's surgery as though he owns it? Changing things, taking over... I could never go back, I *will* never – not even if I'm really sick!"

Thomas might have been deterred by her anger, but Jack was a different character altogether.

"But you were really enjoying helping out there," he insisted. "And I thought you were interested in medicine?"

"No, not really," Ellie said curtly. "Not at all, in fact. It's not as though it did my father much good, is it?" She picked up her spoon again and began to eat quickly, swallowing mouthful after mouthful to signify that the conversation was over.

Jack sighed. He dipped his bread into his bowl and put it into his mouth.

Just then, Charlie picked up his own bowl and upended it over his head, emptying the remains of his soup into his hair with a jubilant squeal.

"Charlie!"

It emerged from Ellie's mouth as a horrified screech, causing Charlie's blue eyes to grow even bigger. She was on her feet in an instant. "You ... you ... how *could* you? Now you'll need another bath and I'll have to wash your clothes ... and they were clean on today. And the table and ... *you!*"

She swung to face Jack, who was almost purple, his hand clamped over his mouth and tears appearing in the corner of his eyes. "It's *not* funny! It's ... you ... oh..."

28

She collapsed back on to her chair, helpless, sobbing laughter choking her throat.

Later as they sat by the fire, Charlie happily splashing in the tub between them, Jack looked across at Ellie, his expression unusually serious.

"I understand why you're angry and upset, El. He was a great man, your dad; a brave man, and it's not right that he was killed."

Ellie used a cup to carefully tip water over Charlie's head, avoiding Jack's eye for fear she would cry again.

"We will win this war – for your pa and all the other good blokes that have been killed or hurt. And I will join up one way or another and help us to victory."

"Jack..." The words stuck in her throat. He was so brave and so loyal, so fierce in defence of those he loved, and he'd been so keen to join the army since the war was first declared. But why didn't he understand that the last thing she wanted was for him to go away too? To leave her and maybe never come back. And for what? Nothing he did would ever bring her father back, or any of the other men... It would only cause more pain.

But she knew better than to argue with Jack. She had hoped and hoped that he would change his mind about joining up, but every passing day, every fresh piece of news about Allied losses or a friend or neighbour who wouldn't be returning only served to make him more determined. It had become less about the adventure and more about what he felt to be his moral duty, and she had to admit a grudging respect for his views – even though she disagreed with them.

She had to accept that they would never agree.

Jack looked a lot older than his fifteen years. He was taller and broader than most boys his age. Ellie had heard of young boys lying and making it to the war underage. She just had to hope that the army recruiters would see through his bravado and refuse to enlist him until he was old enough.

Four

"This is it," Jack shouted. "Wish me luck, El."

"Good luck," she said, and was startled as he lurched forward and seized her in a tight hug.

His face cracked into a grin. "Next time you see me I'll be a real soldier!"

It was mid-October and the army recruiters had returned to Endstone, setting up in the library as they had done when war had first broken out. The war was going on for so much longer than anyone had anticipated and the need for new recruits was greater than ever.

Ellie remembered her father's boyish enthusiasm; he had been first in line to sign up and had made it his personal responsibility to persuade as many local men as possible to follow his example. She swallowed a hard knot in her throat at the memory; it was so vivid. If she closed her eyes she could almost see him there, talking animatedly to men of every age, inspiring them with his bold speeches.

But today it was Jack's eyes that were shining with excitement, his legs jiggling with nerves as he prepared to go in for his interview and medical examination. He was still three years too young to join up officially, but he was determined to give it a try. He had asked Ellie to come along – Charlie with her, of course – for moral support. She had agreed, partly because he was her best friend and she knew how important this was to him, and partly, she told herself, because when they turned him away, she knew he would need cheering up.

As soon as Jack was out of sight, Ellie's smile disappeared. She looked down at Charlie, sitting on the ground, playing with some pebbles he had found. Mother would not be happy to see him sitting in the dirt.

Happily, Mother was far away at the factory.

It felt to Ellie as though all the men of fighting

age from Endstone were already away, either on the battlefields or being trained to join them. But many more had appeared today, including those who had large families to support or important jobs; even those who were married and therefore exempt from conscription. She could almost understand why Jack felt he ought to go; in many ways he was needed less here than some of those queuing to sign up.

It will soon be a village of widows, children and elderly people, Ellie thought. *And men like Thomas, who can't sign up due to their health. How strange that will be.*

"You too, eh, Stan?" called Ellie's neighbour Mr Whitely to his friend Mr Hutchings, who was approaching across the square.

Mr Hutchings' face was anxious but he nodded, pausing to ruffle Charlie's hair as he passed and smile at Ellie. "I don't see as I have a choice any more."

"Quite right. I've just been signed up myself. Perhaps we'll ship out together."

"Perhaps," the other man agreed. His moustache twitched and he chewed his bottom lip. "I can't say I relish the thought of going, to be honest. But it doesn't seem right to stop here any longer when I'm perfectly able to fight."

"I agree, old boy, I agree. I mean, with each chap that comes back injured, not to mention those that don't..." He broke off and both men glanced at Ellie, who tried to look as though she wasn't listening, her gaze fixed on the sea, where a grey mist hung like the chiffon on one of Mother's evening gowns. There would be rain later.

Convinced by her performance, Mr Whitley continued, "And who knows when the whole blasted mess will be over? Oh, look alive, here's trouble..."

Ellie followed their gaze and saw Mrs Hutchings striding across the square towards them, her heels ringing off the cobblestones.

"Now, Lily—" her husband began as she drew close.

"Don't 'now' me, Stanley. I can't believe you were going to do this without even telling me." Her tone was fierce but her whole face spoke of an immense effort not to cry.

"I *was* going to tell you..."

"Afterwards? When it was too late for me to do anything about it?"

Ellie squirmed uncomfortably, but to move away would be to reveal that she had been listening.

"Well..."

"Lily, no one likes this, but we must all help where we can..." Mr Whitely began valiantly.

Mrs Hutchings ignored him. "We're supposed to be a partnership, Stanley. I wouldn't dream of taking such a significant decision without discussing it with you first."

"We *have* discussed it..." her husband replied, but Ellie noticed that his gaze was fixed on the ground, his tone apologetic.

"We haven't *agreed* though, have we?" his wife said softly, reaching a hand out to his shoulder. "Please, Stanley, come home. We can talk about it some more. Please." Her fair hair had tumbled from its pins. She looked a lot younger than she was.

"All right, my darling," Mr Hutchings replied, looking up at last. "All right, I'll come back with you." His wife fell at once into his arms. "Sorry, old boy," he offered to Mr Whitely. His friend shrugged as though to say, "What can one do?"

Ellie watched the Hutchings walk off together, arm

in arm. Would her father have been convinced not to go if she or Mother had tried to stop him? She didn't think so, but they hadn't even attempted, not really. She swallowed a large knot in her throat, feeling the familiar burning sensation in the back of her eyes.

Looking down she realized with shock that Charlie was no longer sitting in front of her. The pebbles were lying abandoned. She spun around, but before she had time to panic she spotted him wobbling up the steps into the library.

"Charlie!" she called, hastening after him.

She ran up the steps and caught him in her arms before he could make it all the way inside. She glanced towards the back of the room where a table was set up with two men in military uniform sitting on one side of it. Jack was facing them with his back to her. She could see from the slump of his shoulders that the news wasn't what he had hoped for. She couldn't help a traitorous lift of her heart, then immediately felt guilty. He would be so disappointed.

Charlie wiggled impatiently in her arms. Ellie turned to go and heard one of the officers say kindly, "I'm sorry it's not the answer you were hoping for, son.

I'm sure you'd make a fine soldier. And, look, maybe *next* year you'll be eighteen? If this wretched war isn't over by then."

Ellie waited for Jack at the bottom of the stairs and, when he emerged, she put her arm around him.

"You heard then?" he said gruffly.

"I'm sorry," was all she said in response.

His mouth quirked up on one side, but there was no real amusement there. "Are you?"

"Yes, I am, Jack, I really am. I don't want you to go, but I know how much it means to you. I don't want you to be unhappy."

He grunted and gently shrugged her off. "Thanks. Anyway, I'd better be getting off home. I'll see you later, El."

"See you later," she echoed sadly, watching him walk off. She hated to see him so dejected. She hated also that the relief that was flooding through her was caused by the very thing that was disappointing him the most.

Later that day, Ellie took Charlie to the village shop to buy tea leaves, sugar and a few other items for the pantry. Jack's mother, Mabel, was engrossed in conversation with Mrs Mertens, the doctor's wife, as they entered. The women's expressions were grave but both smiled warmly in greeting.

"Hello, Ellie! Hello, Charlie!" Jack's mother called.

"Hello, Mabel," said Ellie, then turned to smile shyly at Mrs Mertens, who nodded and waved back. The Belgian lady had a pleasant face, with twinkling eyes and cheeks that dimpled when she smiled, which was often. The Mertens had three children: their eldest, a pretty girl called Sarah who was nineteen; next, thirteen-year-old Camille and finally, ten-year-old Olivier. Ellie didn't know why, but she still felt bashful around Mrs Mertens, and a little wary of the whole family in fact, nice though they seemed.

As Mrs Scott measured out coffee beans for Mrs Mertens, the two ladies resumed their conversation. A newspaper was spread on the counter between them, and both women gestured to it from time to time.

"What a tremendously brave woman!" Mrs Scott exclaimed, shaking her head. "I'd like to think I'd do the same in her position, but I really can't say that I would."

"I know, Mrs Scott," Mrs Mertens replied. Her

English was perfect, with only the slightest hint of an accent. "I quite agree. I have seen the horrors of the war at close hand, have seen the injured soldiers, and been helped out of Belgium myself, but I still don't know that I would have been able to risk my own life – indeed, to sacrifice it – as she did!"

"May I ask who you are speaking about?" Ellie enquired, inching forwards, her curiosity overwhelming her shyness. Still she could not quite meet Mrs Mertens' eye.

"Have you heard about Edith Cavell?" Mrs Scott asked.

Ellie shook her head. She had been so busy minding Charlie and running the house that she couldn't remember the last time she had been able to sit down and read the newspaper. Before Father's death she had pored over it every day, particularly after he had gone away, desperate for a detail that might hint at news about him. It was something that he had always insisted was important. "We must be informed about what is going on outside our own little world in Endstone, Ellie!" he would say. "It is your responsibility to be aware of events elsewhere."

"She was a British nurse, working in Belgium with injured soldiers." Mabel Scott broke into Ellie's thoughts.

"She helped British and French soldiers escape from Belgium." Mrs Mertens took up the story, one hand resting on the paper. "She would shelter them in her own house and then gain them passage to Holland."

A war hero! Ellie thought. *A war hero who was a woman!*

Suddenly a thought occurred to her. "She ... *was* a British nurse?"

The women exchanged a glance.

"The Germans caught her some months ago," Mrs Scott went on. "They found her guilty of treason – that's what they called it – because, according to them, she was helping the enemy. She was executed a few days ago. By a firing squad." Mrs Scott's hand was at her throat; she looked faintly nauseous.

"Oh," Ellie said softly, moving forward to look at the newspaper. She didn't know what else to say.

The two women continued to talk about how all the reports said Edith Cavell had been so brave and dignified, hadn't denied any of the charges against her, nor railed against her fate. As Mrs Mertens completed her purchases, Ellie fetched another copy of the newspaper to take home.

As she made her way across the square, holding Charlie with one hand and clutching the newspaper with the other, she tried to imagine what it must have been like for Edith Cavell, facing a line of men with guns all pointing at her. She wondered how the line of men had felt about it. Her mind winced away from the horror.

Whatever her feelings about the war, she had nothing but admiration for this woman who gave up her life to save others. She couldn't begin to think how someone would become so brave.

Five

Ellie unravelled the thin rope from around the hook on the wall, lowering the clothes line to head height with a screech from the pulley. Charlie was sitting on the floor. As she lowered the line further, he was enveloped in the clean, dry sheets. He squealed with delight, batting at them with his hands and tangling himself up in them.

"Those hands had better be clean," Ellie laughed, gathering the sheets one at a time and loosely folding them ready to be ironed.

When the line was empty – her red-cheeked little brother exposed once more – she reached for the basket of newly washed clothes and began to hang them up.

She was so engrossed in the work and her swirling thoughts, so distracted by Charlie's happy chatter, that she was taken completely by surprise by the sound of the front door opening.

She emerged from behind the hanging clothes in time to see her mother stagger into the room, supported by a plump young woman Ellie did not recognize.

"Mother?" she said in alarm. It was the middle of the day and she hadn't been expecting her mother back for hours. She ran towards her, scooping up Charlie as she went.

Mother did not look well. One hand rested against her chest and her breathing was shallow. Her face looked greyer and more gaunt than ever. Ellie had been annoyed by her mother's pained expression and dramatic silences whenever she returned from the factory, how she would go to bed as soon as she got back, rarely eating anything first. Now she felt a pang of guilt.

"You must be Ellie," the young woman said. "My name's Sally Parkin – I work with your mum. Ooh, and here's the little one." She cooed at Charlie.

The woman was in her early twenties, her mousey

hair pinned back. She too had an unhealthy pallor to her skin, though her dark eyes twinkled brightly.

"Yes, I'm Ellie. It's nice to meet you," she mumbled, jiggling Charlie, who had begun to protest at being restrained. "Mother, are you all right? What happened?"

"She was took poorly, nothing too much to worry about. Probably the chemicals – they don't agree with any of us. Them and the hours we have to work – we're all done in! But your mum – if you don't mind me saying – well, she's not the strongest. She was getting sick and she come over all faint. Even the supervisor could see she wasn't fit for work. Nothing a cup of tea and a bit of rest won't cure, I'm sure. Though – if you don't mind me saying – I'd venture she's not cut out for work in the factory."

While this monologue had been going on, Mother had lowered her head to the table. Ellie deposited Charlie back on to the floor, before moving to her side and putting a hand on her back.

"Should I fetch the doctor?"

"Oh, I shouldn't think so. No, she's a delicate one, your mum, but as I say, it won't kill any of us. Well, at least I hope not!" Her sudden peal of laughter made Ellie jump and even Charlie stared curiously up at her.

"Tea, Eleanor," her mother groaned, still managing to work a note of reproach into her quavering voice.

"Of course, I'm sorry." Ellie started towards the range to pick up the kettle. "You'll have a cup, won't you, Miss Parkin?"

Sally giggled merrily. "Miss Parkin! I don't get called that very often. Though I certainly get called a lot worse. No, thank you, dearie. Much as I'd love a cuppa and a sit down, I'd better be getting back. The supervisor wasn't at all happy about me going with your mum but I said I wasn't sure she'd manage the train alone and I insisted."

"Thank you for taking care of my mother, it's very kind of—"

"Oh, well, if I'm honest – and if you don't mind me saying – I was glad of the break myself," Sally broke in with another loud laugh. "But I don't want to have my wages docked, so I'll be off."

"Thank you again, we're very grateful," said Ellie.

Mother raised her head and nodded weakly in agreement.

"Don't mention it, dearie. And you take care of yourself, Josephine. Hopefully see you back at the factory in a day or two."

Ellie escorted the woman to the door, reeling from the shock of hearing her mother addressed by her first name. She waved her off with more thanks, before returning to the kitchen to rescue the whistling kettle from the stove. Charlie was tugging at their mother's skirt so she swept him up under one arm, *ssssh*ing into his ear as she poured the boiled water over the tea leaves.

"Are you sure you're all right, Mother? Had I better fetch Thomas?"

"Now, don't fuss, Eleanor," Mother said weakly. "You heard the girl. It's no more than we all have to—" She broke off, a hand to her mouth. Ellie watched her anxiously as she stirred sugar into her mother's tea. When she was able to speak again, her mother said, "I must lie down. If you could bring the tea up to me, I would be grateful."

"Of course, Mother."

*

A few hours later Mother emerged back in the kitchen, a shawl wrapped around her shoulders. It made her look so much older and Ellie felt a wave of panic as she set a bowl of thin broth and a plate of bread and butter before her.

"Thank you, Eleanor," Mother said quietly, lifting her spoon and sipping cautiously at the broth.

"Are you feeling any better?" Ellie asked nervously.

"A little, thank you. It is nothing to worry about."

Ellie waited, sensing that this time her mother had more to say. Opposite them Charlie had a piece of bread grasped in his fist. He seemed to have accepted that he wasn't going to get the attention he wanted from his mother and was humming contentedly to himself.

At last Mother continued. "It is just such a *ghastly* place," she whispered, so low that Ellie had to strain to hear her. "We have to stand, for *hours*. It's exhausting. We hardly get any breaks at all and I often feel as though I might faint. And I'm not the only one, despite what you might think about my capabilities."

Ellie began to protest, but her mother spoke over her, her voice commanding attention despite its softness.

"There is no fresh air; the place is thick with powder and chemicals. Some of those who have been working there longer look yellow from all the sulphur."

Ellie had noticed some people about the village with a yellowish tinge to their complexion but hadn't associated it with the factory, nor with the nickname "canary" which she had heard without understanding it. The poorer villagers, she had assumed, were suffering more than the others from the restricted diet the war had brought about. With a sickening jolt she thought of Jack. He had been looking a little jaundiced lately, but as he always seemed so full of health and vigour, she had explained it to herself as the sallow remains of his summer tan.

She looked again at her mother, spooning the tiny mouthfuls of broth to her lips. If even someone as robust as Jack was suffering, how on earth could Mother expect to cope?

"Sometimes," her mother added, "we are allowed to take a nap, if we can find somewhere quiet. And clean." Ellie tried and failed to imagine her mother curling up in the corner of a busy factory. "But we all have a quota we must fulfil. And I..." She scowled at Ellie as though in anticipation of some imagined criticism. "Well, I struggle to keep up with some of the younger, stronger women as it is."

A quota? Ellie thought. *What happens if they don't meet their quota?* She remembered Sally saying that her wages would be docked if she didn't hurry back.

"Oh, and I know it's necessary, and we must all do our bit, but it's just so shameful. And the other women, well, they're hardly our sort..."

Ellie felt her sympathy give way to a familiar flicker of irritation. Trust her mother to find fault with the other women. Clearly they should have been the least of her concerns.

This irritation helped give voice to the feelings bubbling up inside her.

"Mother, I just don't understand why you're doing it. Yes, I know we must all help out where we can, but you simply are not built for this sort of work. Anyone can see that." Mother opened her mouth, but it was Ellie's turn to speak over her. "There is no need to be a martyr. It's clear you can't cope!" Her mother's eyes widened, but Ellie refused to be stopped. "I only have one parent now and I'd like you to remain healthy!"

She stopped. Both their mouths slammed shut; mother and daughter equally shocked by what had been said.

"Eleanor..." Mother began, but seemed unsure how to continue. "It is not just ... it is not simply... You don't seem to understand. With Father gone..."

Ellie blinked. There *was* more to Mother's sudden urge to work than patriotism, she knew it!

"I haven't wanted to say anything before ... but we need an income!" Mother burst out, looking deeply unhappy at having to speak so openly.

For a second time today, Ellie was stunned – and she felt stupid at not having realized it before. Her mother's cheeks had a hint of pinkness in their pallor. She glared down at the tablecloth and Ellie hovered uncertainly, wanting to comfort her but sure she would be rebuffed.

At the same time, she felt the beginnings of an idea seed itself in her mind.

"Mother..." Her mother raised her eyes slowly. "Isn't it true that there are some younger women at the factory? Some nearly as young as me?"

"What of it?" Mother asked, her eyes narrowing.

"Well ... why don't I go to work in the factory in your place? I could earn money for us!" Mother winced but Ellie ploughed on. "I could probably earn more!" And she'd get to see Jack more, she thought, but knew better than to share that sentiment.

"Stop it, Eleanor! There is no excuse for being so vulgar! And don't be ridiculous; of course you can't go to work. You are only a child!"

"But Mother—"

"I said no, Eleanor, and let that be an end to it! What do you suppose your father would think of me sending his fourteen-year-old daughter to work in the factory? With girls of that sort?"

"I hardly see why he would find it worse than you going! And it sounds as though I'd be much better suited to the work than you. You could stay here with Charlie. You see how he misses you..."

Ellie thought she saw a flicker of something pass across her mother's face, but it was gone a second later, replaced with a look of extreme weariness.

"Eleanor, please. I said no and I mean it. I don't want to argue with you. I'm exhausted enough as it is."

Chastened, Ellie said meekly, "Sorry, Mother. Try

to have a little more of the broth. You need to get your strength up."

Ellie was emptying the water from Charlie's bath out into the garden when she was surprised by a shout from the path. Living on the edge of the village, the Phillips got few passers-by. Looking up, she saw Jack's younger brother, George, swinging on the garden gate, his reddish-blonde curls poking out from under his flat cap and a grin on his face.

"Hello, George!" she exclaimed. "It's lucky for you I've just tucked Charlie up in bed or he'd never let you leave."

"Hmm." George frowned a little; he didn't always enjoy Charlie's enthusiastic attentions.

"What brings you up here?"

"I was at Ollic's," George replied, jerking a thumb over his shoulder. For the first time, Ellie noticed the Mertens' youngest son Olivier standing behind him. He waved and smiled; he had dark hair and eyes but his flat cap and mischievous expression matched George's perfectly.

"Oh, hello, Olivier."

"Hello, Miss Phillips."

"Anyway," George interrupted impatiently. "I thought you'd like to know – we've had a message from Will!"

"Oh? That's good." Will was the Scotts' oldest son. He had gone away to war at the same time as Ellie's father. Ellie was always glad for her friends when they heard from him, but she couldn't help a pang of envy that Will was alive when her father wasn't.

"Yes, and guess what?"

Ellie shook her head.

"He's coming home on leave! He'll be back in Endstone in a couple of days!"

Six

Will greeted Ellie warmly and steered her to a seat at the kitchen table, where she was plied with tea and home-made bread and jam. The atmosphere at the Scotts' house could not have been more different from that of her own. With all of them home, the tiny house seemed crammed to bursting; the noise of happy chatter spilling out on to the street.

"Ellie," Will said seriously, once she was settled with a heaped plate and steaming cup in front of her, "I was so very sorry to hear about Dr Phillips. He was the best of men and I feel honoured to have known him."

Ellie nodded her thanks, not trusting herself to speak.

She studied Will while she tried to regain her

composure. He had always been slighter, quieter and shier than Jack. Now he seemed older and more tired-looking, but also more confident. His family hung around him adoringly – all except their father, Joe, who was nowhere to be seen. For once, Will was the centre of the stories. Mabel Scott looked happier than Ellie had seen her in a long time. She hovered around the edge of the kitchen, offering drinks and food and finding any excuse to rest her hand on her eldest son's back or brush an imaginary bit of fluff from his uniform.

"Oh, but they're a great bunch of lads," Will was saying now. "Really, the best in the world!"

Ellie thought of her father's letters, which had said similar things. She swallowed the thick lump in her throat.

Will told of how they planned battle strategies, shared treats from home and stole letters that other lads had received from their sweethearts to read aloud in simpering tones. He talked about playing practical jokes on each other, though never on the officers, who sounded rather more intimidating.

"Sounds to me like you're all having a blooming

holiday out there while we slave away!" Jack exclaimed. He was laughing, but Ellie could hear the envy in his voice and she was sure his brother could too.

Will laughed as well. "We haven't done much actual fighting yet, it's true. I don't mind admitting, I'm rather pleased." He glanced at Ellie.

She smiled back at him, relieved. She had had mixed feelings about coming to the Scotts' today, not least because her mother still wasn't back at the factory and had never approved of them. But she had wanted to see Will. She'd missed his kind and steadying presence, at the same time dreading what horrible details of the trenches she might hear; details that would feed into her nightmares, into her endless, obsessive imagining of what her father had gone through in the last few months of his life.

"It was a lark picking George up from school earlier," Will said, smiling, still watching Ellie carefully.

"Oh, it was sickening," Anna Scott broke in, laughing. "You should have seen the fuss they all made of him, Ellie!"

Ellie smiled back. "The little boys?"

"Not just them! The girls! The teachers! Everyone! It's a good job he's not sticking around long; it would go straight to his head and he'd end up like our Jack!"

"Oi!" Jack tugged on the end of her thick red braid. "The world would be a better place if everyone were more like your Jack!"

"I brought an enemy helmet for them all to see," Will added. "I thought George would enjoy showing it off to his mates."

"I did," George agreed, his head nodding vigorously under the helmet and making them all laugh even more.

Ellie looked at Jack, who was sitting beside his older brother and hanging off his every word. He'd never paid much attention to Will before he went to war. Back then he had always been so frustrated by Will's cautious, measured ways. They looked more alike now too. Will had filled out a little and he held himself differently; less apologetically, somehow.

Will grinned at his brother and punched him lightly on the arm. "There's a boy out there – young lad – reminds me so much of you, Jack. I've told him so."

"Handsome chap, is he? Brave and dashing and all that?"

"Full of nonsense, more like." The brothers grappled playfully for a moment but then Will's face became serious again. "You were right though, Jack. You'd make a great soldier. You've got guts; you're not afraid to do what needs to be done. You've no idea how important that is – or how rare."

"Course I was right," Jack blustered, but his cheeks glowed with pleasure and he seemed to grow a few inches before their eyes.

"Don't you go encouraging him in that soldier business," Mabel admonished her eldest, hands once again on his shoulders. "He's bad enough as it is."

"Thinks highly enough of himself as it is, you mean," Anna said and earned another yank of her plait.

"Anyway, that's enough about me. I want to hear everything I've missed here. Ellie, I hear there's a new doctor in your dad's surgery. A Belgian refugee, is that right? Father of little George's new mate?"

"I'm not little," George put in but was ignored.

"Yes," Ellie answered dismissively. "But I'm glad to

see you're not injured, Will, so you won't have to be treated by him. By all accounts he's a bumbling fool and you'll come out of the surgery more ill than when you went in." She added a brash laugh, but a glance at the faces of the Scotts revealed identical shock at the savagery of her tone – except for George, who had lost interest in the conversation now that it had turned away from battle and trenches.

Anna and Mabel exchanged a look and moved away to the stove, busying themselves with preparing the evening meal. Will's gaze fell to his hands, his cheeks colouring. Inevitably it was Jack who tackled Ellie.

"What rot! By whose accounts would this be?"

Ellie felt her cheeks burning. "Well..."

"And I don't know how you'd have the first clue about it, Ellie Phillips," he continued. "You haven't set foot in the surgery for months, despite Dr Pritchard begging for your help." His tone was teasing but it wounded her nonetheless. She glared back at him, her mind scrabbling for a response that would put him in his place.

Will saved her. "Shut up, Jack, or I'll change my

mind about you making a good soldier. You know, that kind of talk to the wrong person can get you killed."

The brothers looked at Ellie's furious expression and burst out laughing.

Ellie tried to carry on scowling but after a moment gave in and allowed herself a smile.

"Despite what Ellie would have you believe," Jack continued, "Dr Mertens and his family are very nice and they're settling in well. They're proper Endstone locals now. Their oldest daughter Sarah is even being courted by Dr Pritchard!"

"Rubbish!" Ellie exploded, her anger blazing back. "Just because they've sat next to each other a few times in church! That's only polite when her father is his colleague. How on earth does that mean they're courting?"

"Oh, keep your hair on!" Jack replied. "That's not what our Anna has heard, anyway."

"Shush, Jack," Anna mumbled from by the sink, where she was peeling potatoes. "Leave me out of this."

"And I wouldn't blame him if they *were* courting," Jack went on, never one to be easily silenced. "She's very pretty."

Ellie's scowl deepened.

"Is she indeed?" Will was asking. "Hold a bit of a candle for her, do you, Jack?"

"Wait till you see her, Will. Long, shining, dark hair. Enormous brown eyes. Any man would."

"Oh, and you're a man now, are you?"

"As you see..."

They continued to joke and tease each other. Ellie rose to her feet and moved towards the door.

"Oh, don't be like that, El!" Jack protested.

"Be like what?" Ellie asked, smiling thinly. "I need to get back in case Mother wakes and wants me. It was lovely to see you, Will. I'm glad you're well. I'm sure I'll see you again before you go."

"You will, you will," he agreed. "Wonderful to see you too, Ellie. Please send my regards to your mother and young Charlie."

"Of course," Ellie lied. She couldn't pass on his regards without revealing to her mother that she had been here, which she wasn't about to do if she could help it.

"And mine," Mabel said, wiping her hands on her apron. "Here, take this." She handed Ellie a jar of her home-made blackberry jam. "Now, don't argue. I know how your Charlie loves it."

"He does," Ellie admitted. "Thank you." It always made her squirm to think how generous the Scotts were when they had so little.

After several more goodbyes, she finally left. Despite the warmth and kindness of the Scotts, despite having laughed more that evening than she had done in months, Ellie found herself stomping back across the square, her brow still furrowed. Once again, frost was settling on the cobblestones and darkness was drawing in. She drew her coat about her and sighed as she noticed the frayed cuffs. All the clothing she owned was looking tattered and worn; that was, if it even fitted her. So many of her skirts were too short now; her blouses too tight.

It was all well and good for Sarah Mertens to look pretty, she fumed. All she seemed to do was sit around at the surgery. That was nothing like chasing around after a filthy toddler, or shopping, cooking, cleaning, bathing, gardening...

Still, Ellie had to admit to herself, her furious pace slowly slightly, that these differences alone didn't explain how Sarah Mertens always looked so smart, so perfect. Goodness knew, the Mertens were refugees and couldn't have much money. Sarah didn't seem to have lots of clothes, so it was puzzling that the few she did have were always neat and tidy...

Clearly this was what Mother meant about the importance of needlework, not to mention taking better care of one's things. Ellie sighed. Two of her dresses still fitted her well enough and had been nice before they had succumbed to moths and fraying hems. Perhaps she should dig them out and see what she might do to make them more presentable. Just because there was a war on, it didn't mean she had to wander around looking like a scarecrow...

Ellie grimaced, before pulling her coat around her once more and trudging up the path to home.

Since when had she started to think like her mother?

Seven

Ellie rinsed the last of the breakfast cups and put it to drain on the rack. As she looked up from the sink she saw Thomas limping up the garden path. The ground was twinkling with December frost and the doctor was bundled up in a warm coat, hat and scarf, his feet crunching noisily against the hard ground. Ellie smiled at the sight of him. She rarely saw him these days. She had long since apologized for her outburst, but despite missing his company, she still found herself avoiding the surgery.

Her smile wavered slightly as she noticed his grave expression. She hurried to the door to let him in.

"Thomas! How nice to see you. Come in, please."

She reached out to take his coat then ushered him to a seat by the stove.

"Thank you, Ellie. I will, though I can't stay long; I must get to the surgery." His kind eyes regarded her carefully. "I just thought you'd want to know as soon as possible."

Ellie's stomach began to roil like the sea at Big Beach on a stormy day. "Know what?"

"It's Jack," he began. Glancing at her expression he hesitated, then hurriedly continued, "Don't worry, he's perfectly well as far as I know. But I was in The Dog and Duck last night and Joe Scott – who had been drinking rather too much again, I'm sorry to say – was telling everyone that Jack has run away to war with his brother."

Ellie dropped the kettle on to the stove with a clatter.

"Yes, I didn't think you could have known," Thomas went on apologetically. "I got Joe on his own later and he said that he and the boys' mother believe the older lad – Will, isn't it? – must have somehow got hold of a spare uniform for Jack and helped him forge some papers. Very irresponsible of him, I must say."

"That's not like Will," Ellie breathed, turning to stare out of the window. It was all she could think of to say. Thomas's words were battering away at the outside of her brain like moths around a lamp, desperate to get in but making no headway.

"Ellie? Are you all right? This must be a terrible shock."

"When—" Her voice came out as a whisper. She cleared her throat and tried again. "When did they leave?"

"Yesterday morning – very early, I believe. They caught an earlier train than Will had told his mother he'd be taking. They were gone before the rest of the family was up."

"Oh, Mabel," Ellie murmured.

"Quite," agreed Thomas. "That poor woman. I imagine she is beside herself. According to Mr Scott, Will left a note insisting that he would take good care of his brother and that they would both be home again in no time."

Ellie snorted, then blew her nose noisily on her handkerchief.

"Yes, I don't imagine that was much consolation to

their family either. I'm terribly sorry to have to deliver such bad news, Ellie, I really am."

"It's quite all right, Thomas," Ellie said with a briskness she wished she felt. "It isn't your fault." She hurried into the hallway and took her coat from the cupboard.

Thomas followed her. "Where are you going?"

"I must go to see Mabel... To see if there's anything..." She trailed off, unsure of what she could really offer Jack's family. But they were the only people she wanted to see at that moment.

"But Charlie..."

"He can stay here while I run down to the shop. Mother's upstairs. She still hasn't gone back to the factory."

Thomas gave her a searching look.

"Honestly, Thomas, I'm fine. It's not as though Jack didn't give all of us plenty of warning that he would do something of this sort. He was so frustrated he wasn't allowed to sign up by the official route... And didn't you say you had to be getting to the surgery, anyway?"

Thomas shook his head as though coming back to

himself. "Yes, you're right. Well, please do give my best to Mrs Scott. And if there's anything I can do..."

"Of course, Thomas, I'll let you know." Ellie bustled him out of the door before dashing upstairs to tell her mother that she was running down to the village to pick up some groceries. She hurried away before her mother had a chance to object.

Without stopping to pull her bicycle from the shed, she sped down the steep path into village. The icy wind streamed over her, ripping angry tears from her eyes.

How could he?

How *could* he?

She wasn't looking at the path, so it shouldn't have come as a surprise that her foot landed awkwardly on a loose stone and sent her tumbling on to her hands and knees.

"Stupid, stupid, stupid," she spat, picking herself back up and brushing the grit from her bloodied hands. Her stockings were torn. She would have to patch them up before Mother saw. They would soon be more patch than stocking.

Five minutes later, she staggered into the village shop, making the bell on the door clang angrily. Mabel and Anna Scott glanced up as she walked in. They both looked worn and weary. Mabel's eyes filled instantly with tears, but Anna drew herself up and stretched her mouth into a grim smile.

"You've heard, then?" she said, her voice seeming loud in the still of the shop.

Ellie nodded, moving closer.

"Don't look like that," Anna continued, chin raised defiantly. "No one's died."

All three winced.

"No, I know," Ellie said falteringly. "I know. I'm sorry..."

"We knew it was coming, didn't we?" Anna said, softening slightly. "He's been talking about it long enough."

Ellie nodded again.

"It's true," Mabel said, reaching out and rubbing Ellie's shoulder. "It was getting worse; he was talking about it all the time. I knew really..." Her voice wobbled. "I knew he wouldn't be happy until he'd done it. And it seems he and Will had been planning it for a while."

"Yes." Anna took up the story again. "I thought it was odd that Will was sending all these long letters

69

just for Jack. It made me cross – it didn't seem fair! Otherwise he just wrote letters for all of us to share, apart from a little note for me on my birthday."

It was true then, Ellie thought. Jack had been planning it for ages. And he'd never said anything, even though she had gone with him when he tried to join up! Even when they saw each other a few days ago. He knew all along that he was going!

She stared hard at the floor, her eyes burning, feeling the gaze of the two Scott women on her.

She looked up and forced a smile. "Well, I'm proud of him!" she said brightly. Her voice sounded thick, even to her own ears, but she carried on regardless. "I'm proud of him and you must be too! He's a hero, just like Will. He didn't let anything stop him."

If only she meant it, she thought.

How could he have left without telling her?

That evening after she'd cleaned up the dinner things and finally got Charlie and her mother settled in their beds, Ellie gazed out of the kitchen window again. She was alone with her thoughts for the first time since the morning, and she found that she couldn't bear them.

Throwing on her warm things, she stomped out of the house and wrestled her bicycle from the shed. It was very dark but she knew the paths around the village well. She just needed to be out.

She swung a leg over the saddle and then stopped. Something pale, gleaming in the spokes of the front wheel, caught her eye. She leaned forward and snatched it up: an envelope. She could barely make out the words in the dim light spilling from the house, but she knew the round, childish hand at once.

Dropping the bicycle, she clattered back into the house and dropped into a seat at the kitchen table without even loosening her scarf. She tore open the envelope and pulled out the note. Seeing his carefully printed letters pushed her anger back for the first time that day. Into its place rushed sadness. And fear.

Dear Ellie,

Well, I know you'll be annoyed with me and I'm sorry. I really am. I hope you find this soon, but all the same I expect you'll already know by the time you read it that I've gone away to war with Will.

I wanted to tell you I was going so many times,

even though I know you'd tell me not to. But I didn't want to get you into trouble.

I couldn't wait three years, El. Please try to be proud of me, it would mean so much if you could. I just want to be a proper man like your dad, to fight for my country and to sort out those bullying Germans.

I know you'll be worried, but I promise I'll be home soon. Believe me.

Please think of me and keep me in your prayers. Take care of yourself, El. I'll miss you and be thinking of you always.

Love,

Jack

Ellie read the letter over and over, remembering with a jolt how she had done the same with her father's letters.

She pushed it away and lowered her head to her arms, finally allowing herself to give in to tears.

Not again, she thought to herself. *Oh, please, please not again.*

Eight

Waiting, she thought to herself. *Always waiting for good news. Or bad.*

Ellie was at the kitchen sink once more, watching the postman Mr Berry toiling up the hill to the garden gate, while her heart tried to escape through the wall of her throat. She felt as though she were living the hardest times in her life again and again.

When she eventually met the postman at the door, however, she could see at once that the letter he handed over was not from Jack. The envelope was written in a neater, more adult hand, and addressed to Mrs Wesley Phillips. Seeing her father's name made exchanging pleasantries with Mr Berry challenging, and she was glad when eventually he was gone.

And then here she was once again, sitting opposite her mother at the kitchen table, waiting impatiently for her to finish reading.

Waiting. Again. It's the worst kind of torture.

When Mother eventually raised her head, Ellie saw that her eyes were rimmed with red. She didn't say a word; merely pushed the letter across the table to Ellie, who seized it eagerly.

Dear Mrs Wesley Phillips and family,

Please allow me to introduce myself. My name is Albert Murphy and I served in the same battalion as your late husband in France.

I want to convey first and foremost my deepest sympathies and regret at the loss of your husband and father. He was a wonderful man; kind, honourable and brave – as I experienced first hand.

I know something of the telegrams a family receives from the army in sad situations such as yours, and can well imagine that they don't go nearly far enough in telling you what you want to know. I hope very much that what I have to share will bring some comfort to you, and I beg your forgiveness for any fresh sadness it may raise.

As you will know, your husband, despite his medical responsibilities within the army, was often in the trenches, feeling that this was where he could do the most good. I hardly need to tell you that this was typical of him; always thinking selflessly of how he could be of the greatest use. On that terrible day, I went over the top and was shot down pretty well immediately by the enemy. I was caught on the barbed wire so couldn't even crawl back to the trench. None of the others could help me – even if they'd seen what had happened. But Wesley had seen from the trench and he jumped out and helped untangle me from the wire and staunched some of the worst of the bleeding from the gunshot wounds. He had just got me back to the trench when was shot himself and, as I'm sure you have been told, killed instantly.

So, as you see, I owe my life to your husband – something I will think of and be grateful for every single day that remains to me. So too will my family. I am married with six children, and please believe me that every one of us has Wesley in our daily prayers. We are sadder than we can say that his heroic act has resulted in your great loss.

My own return home and recovery have been very slow, which is the reason for the tardiness of this letter. I will never be able to use my left arm again, which excuses me from further military duty. I am all too aware of how very lucky I am, and how much worse things might – would – have been, were it not for your husband.

He always seemed a very humble man – indeed, he seemed entirely unaware that there was anything special about him at all! – so I doubt his own letters will have conveyed to you how well respected and loved he was among the men. In particular, the younger soldiers saw him as a father figure while they were so far from home. One story I think of often, and have told my own children, was how he came across a distressed horse, removed a thorn from its hoof with his medical tweezers and then insisted on finding and returned it to its owner.

I have many more such stories I could share. Please don't hesitate to let me know if you have any

76

more questions about Wesley's time in the army, or
indeed if there is anything I or my family can do to
be of assistance to you during this sad time.

In the meantime, please be assured that I am
yours sincerely,

Albert Murphy

Ellie hadn't even noticed the tears flowing down her cheeks. When she looked up at last, she saw that her mother had left the room. Ellie thought about going after her, but decided against it. Mother rarely seemed to want any comfort that Ellie might offer.

Besides, her own mind was jittering about, her stomach clenching. She refolded the letter and set it down the table, before hurrying up the stairs and flinging herself on to her bed.

Not fair, not fair, not fair... The thought rattled through her brain. *Why should Albert Murphy's children have their father when Charlie and I don't have ours? Why should he be a father figure to the younger men instead of being home with his own children? Why couldn't he just stay in the trench as anyone else would have done? Why did he always have*

to be the hero? How can Mr Murphy live with himself,
knowing Father died in his place?

Hot tears leaked on to her pillow, the blanket
bunched in her fist.

She could hear Charlie chattering away in their
mother's room.

Ellie didn't know how long she'd been lying there –
she couldn't even say for certain that she'd been awake
the whole time – but she realized that she'd stopped
crying. Her mind was calmer now, as she rehearsed the
details of the letter.

She sat up and scrubbed at her eyes.

Before she knew what she was doing, she found
herself back downstairs at the kitchen table, the letter in
her hands. She read it again. She realized she was smiling,
thinking about her father tending to the injured horse.
That was so like him. And she might never had heard
that story if it weren't for Mr Murphy. She smoothed the
letter down as her eyes roamed over it once more.

There was still no sign of Mother. Ellie drew a deep
breath. A walk. That was what she needed. She would
take Charlie into the village. She splashed her face at
the kitchen sink and then went to fetch him.

Once they were both wrapped up in their warm clothes, they set off down the path into the village. Now Charlie was bigger and steadier on his legs, Ellie preferred to leave the pram at home and hold him tightly by the hand, even though, more often than not, she would end up chasing him as he broke free.

This happened now as they reached the square and Charlie caught sight of the Christmas tree. Wrenching his hand from hers, he set off towards it at a trot.

Ellie followed behind.

The tree was humbler than those of previous years; smaller and scantily draped with decorations that were either home-made or leftover from past Christmases. That didn't stop Charlie from gazing at it with an awestruck grin on his face.

As she drew level with him, she realized that he was not alone: the two younger Mertens children, Camille and Olivier, were also standing by the tree, listening politely to Charlie's infant babble about presents and Father Christmas and sweeties.

"Hello," Ellie said shyly to the other children, when Charlie paused for breath. She had scarcely seen them since she had stopped going to school, and even before then, hadn't spoken to them much.

"Hello, Ellie." Camille and Olivier both smiled broadly at her.

"Sorry about Charlie, he loves an audience and doesn't seem to mind whether or not they're interested."

Camille laughed. "Not at all, he's very informative. And, actually, it's nice to talk to someone else in the village who doesn't speak perfect English!"

It was Ellie's turn to laugh, though, in truth, the younger girl's English had improved almost beyond recognition since they had last spoken. Ellie wondered if she herself would be able to learn another language so quickly, all while trying to settle into an entirely new place with new people.

As though reading her mind, Olivier said, "We were just saying, it feels a little strange to be far from home at this time of year." His English was strangely formal for the mischievous ten year old she knew him to be.

"Yes," Camille continued. "Everyone in Endstone has been so kind and welcoming, but we can't help but miss our friends from home, and think about what we would be doing if we were there. Or at least, what we would have been doing before the war."

Ellie's cheeks felt hot. She could not really claim to have been kind and welcoming to the Mertens. "This war ruins everything," she agreed. "But I can't even imagine what it must be like for you. I'm ... I'm sorry."

"Why, Ellie?" Camille's cheeks dimpled like her mother's when she smiled. "You have nothing to be sorry for."

"I know the tree doesn't look like much," Ellie went on in a rush, "and I know it can't ever replace your home, but Christmas in Endstone is very nice, I promise. The whole village goes to church in the morning – even the people who don't usually – and there are carols. And then afterwards lots of the grown-ups go to The Dog and Duck and everybody else gathers in the square before going home for dinner. And there are candles everywhere and wreaths..."

"What are wreaths?" Camille asked.

"Oh, they're a kind of decoration, made from branches and twigs and things from trees. We hang them on our front doors at Christmas time. They're very pretty."

"Oh, yes, I think I know these."

"I'll make you one," Ellie said hurriedly. "I'll bring it to your house. You're just by the surgery, aren't you?" She blushed again. She knew well where they lived, though she had never visited.

"That would be very kind, Ellie. Very kind. Thank you." Camille smiled so warmly Ellie felt more ashamed than ever.

The Mertens said their goodbyes and Ellie settled on to a bench to watch Charlie run back and forth across the square. She *would* make them a wreath, she decided. Straight away. She felt unsettled by all the changes in Endstone, but it was *still* Endstone. It was still her home. She couldn't begin to think how strange things must be for these children, so far from their home.

How quickly another Christmas was approaching.

She remembered last year, how they had been so desperate to see Father, and then – when they learned he wouldn't be home for Christmas – just to have word from him. And of course the news had come so soon afterwards. This year it would be Jack she was waiting to hear from.

Let him be safe, she thought urgently. *Just please let him be safe.*

Nine

Ellie selected a last few items from the shelves of the village shop – some chocolate and a packet of OXO cubes for making the turkey gravy – and then returned to the counter, where Anna Scott was packing up the rest of her groceries. Ellie couldn't help but notice that she was being rougher than usual as she thrust them into the paper bags. She winced as a carton of eggs was shoved in with particular savagery.

"I suppose you'll want these put on your bill?" Anna snapped.

Ellie was taken aback by her tone. "Um ... yes, please. If that's all right?"

"Does it make any difference if it isn't?" came the cutting reply.

"I don't ... I don't know what you mean."

Anna lowered her voice a little, but Ellie was still painfully aware of how it carried through the busy shop. "Ellie, you must know your bill is enormous. It's high time you paid it off. We're not unreasonable – we know everyone's struggling – but we're hardly flush with money ourselves."

"Anna," Mabel's voice came warningly as she emerged from the store room.

"Well, it's true, Mam. We can't afford to be—"

"Anna! Stop!"

"No, it's all right, Mabel. Of course we must pay it," Ellie stammered, feeling several pairs of eyes burning into her back and wanting nothing more than to run from the shop. "I'm so sorry. I didn't realize—" She broke off, not wanting to speak badly of her mother, who was already unpopular in the village. Twin currents of anger and shame were bubbling up inside her.

"It's quite all right, dear," Mabel said gently, "we know you'll pay just as soon as you can."

Anna made a scornful noise but fell silent at a look from her mother.

"We ... I will. Straight away." Ellie gathered up the offending packages, and hurried from the shop without meeting anyone else's eyes.

She ran all the way home, her hands too full to wipe the angry tears from her eyes. She had no idea the bill was so large and hadn't been paid. She supposed, thinking about it now, she ought to have guessed. She knew things had become tight, even before Father went away to war. And Mother was still not back at work... But Ellie couldn't believe her mother had been allowing this to happen. How could she live with the shame?

She burst through the door and into the kitchen, causing her mother, who was sitting at the table with a cup of tea, to jump.

"Goodness, Eleanor, one would think *you* were a soldier with the amount of grace you have. Or a factory worker!"

"Well, perhaps you should let me be one – a factory worker, I mean," Ellie said as she slammed the bags down by the sink.

"Please do not start that again. And calm yourself. Whatever has got you into such a state?"

"Mother, why didn't you tell me we had such a large unpaid bill at the shop?"

Mother took a deep breath before she replied. "Well, really, Eleanor, that's none of your concern."

"It *is* my concern," Ellie said through gritted teeth, "when I'm the one who gets shamed in front of the Scotts and everyone else in the village. Why didn't you say something?"

"Honestly, Eleanor, I really think sometimes you forget which of us is the parent! Kindly do not take that tone with me! We're getting by. And we don't have much choice, anyway, while I'm unable to work."

"But, Mother, if you would just let me—"

"Eleanor, I have said no. I do not wish to discuss it again. For once, could you accept a decision of mine? Now, my headache is worse. I'm going to lie down."

Her mother left the room and Ellie slumped into a seat at the table, leaving the brown paper shopping bags untouched on the side.

Oh, Jack, she thought. *If only you were here.* Jack could always cheer her up, whatever else was going on. She couldn't remember a time they'd been apart for so long in all the years of their friendship.

86

She did not have long to dwell on Jack.

"Eleanor," her mother called from upstairs.

Ellie clomped slowly up the stairs and stood in the doorway of her mother's room.

Mother lay stiffly in the bed, propped up by pillows, her eyes closed and a hand to her forehead. The window was slightly open, allowing an icy draught into the room. Ellie shifted uncomfortably but said nothing.

"Eleanor," Mother said at last in a thin voice, "my headache is unbearable. I need you to go to the surgery and pick up a prescription from Thomas for me."

Ellie's hand went to her suddenly churning stomach and rubbed it distractedly. "Couldn't ... I mean, mightn't I..." She trailed off, unable to find words for her sudden confusion.

Mother opened one eye and looked at her incredulously. "Is even this small request too much to ask, Eleanor?" Her voice seemed to have risen an octave.

"No, no," Ellie said hastily. "Of course not. I'll go now."

"*Thank* you," her mother replied in a tone that suggested no gratitude, closing both eyes again.

Glancing out of the window as she buttoned up her coat, Ellie decided that it was too icy for her bicycle. She took her time lacing and re-lacing her boots, checking on Charlie and tidying away stray items in the kitchen, but at last it could be put off no longer, and she set off down the path to the surgery.

It felt so long since she had last been this way. With every step her boots seemed to weigh more heavily on her feet. The hedgerows around her were dark, bare, jagged with branches, the occasional evergreen – so dark as to appear almost black – twining through them, dotted with berries.

Finally she reached the small surgery building. She stood on the step, looking at the dark-blue front door and the familiar brass knocker. When Father had been here, she had barged straight into the waiting room. Now she felt she ought to knock. It wasn't her place any more; she had no claim to it.

She stood, every muscle tensed, her jaw clenched tight, staring fixedly at the knocker. Eventually the cold creeping into her bones became intolerable.

"Come *along*," she said to herself crossly.

Before she had time to think any further, she took

hold of the knocker and rapped it sharply against the wood.

All too quickly, the door swung open and Thomas stood before her. At the sight of her, his eyes widened and one corner of his mouth crept upwards.

"Ellie!" he exclaimed. "It's ... well, it's wonderful to see you. Come in, come in. You know you never have to knock."

He ushered her into the waiting room, his hand warm on her back. There were no patients in the reception area and the small table was set with tea things. Sarah Mertens was pouring from the teapot. She looked up as Ellie entered and gave her a warm smile.

"Oh!" Ellie said. "I'm sorry, I don't want to interrupt." She made to take a step back, but Thomas was still behind her, his hand pressing her gently but firmly forwards.

"Don't be silly. You know you will always be welcome here. We were just taking advantage of the lull. You know Miss Mertens, don't you?"

Ellie nodded awkwardly.

"We have met," the young woman confirmed, her

smile stretching even wider. "But, please, you must call me Sarah. I often visit my father here."

"Won't you sit down?" Thomas asked Ellie.

"Yes, do! As you can see, we were just about to have some tea. Please will you join us?" Sarah had only the slightest trace of an accent. Her voice was surprisingly deep. She sounded as though she were rolling the words around her tongue, enjoying the taste of them.

Glancing back at Thomas, Ellie realized there was something was different about him. His shirt, normally wrinkled and untucked, was neatly ironed; his hair newly cut.

Feeling surer than ever that she was interrupting, Ellie said quickly, "No, thank you, but I won't stay. Thomas, my mother is unwell with one of her headaches and she was hoping you could write her a prescription."

Thomas's eyes searched her face but all he said was, "Of course."

As he went to fetch his prescription pad from the desk in the corner, Sarah said, "It is a wonderful place that your father set up here. You must be very proud."

Ellie chewed on her lip and nodded again. She didn't trust herself to speak.

"He must have been a brilliant man. Everyone says he was. Thomas speaks of him so often, I feel as though I knew him myself." Her smile was softer now, her large brown eyes regarding Ellie kindly. "Would you ... would you like to see his consulting room?"

Ellie felt a wave of panic rising and took another involuntary step backwards.

Sarah's hand reached out, but did not quite touch her. "Please, my father and Thomas work in there now, of course, but I think you would like to see it..."

Ellie found herself following Sarah's delicate figure down the corridor and into the room in which she had spent so many hours with her father. The familiar smell assailed her and she had to stop and close her eyes for a moment.

When she opened them she felt as though she had stepped back in time.

Everything in the room was exactly as it had been the last time she had seen it. She drew in a breath.

"You see?" Sarah said, her voice barely more than a whisper. "They have left it just as it was."

"Of course," came Thomas's voice from behind them. "Wesley ran things perfectly. Why would we change anything?"

To her surprise, Ellie felt a small smile on her lips. She remembered how baffling Thomas had found her father's systems when he was first handling them alone. She was just about to remind him of this, but stopped at the sound of the front door opening.

It was Dr Mertens, manoeuvring his portly form through the narrow hallway with surprising grace.

"Thomas," he began, before breaking off. "Oh, hello, Miss Phillips, how good to see you here." His accent was strong, but he spoke perfectly good English, as Thomas had said. "I would love to stay and drink tea with you but I'm afraid Thomas and I are needed rather urgently."

Thomas looked up, his brow creased.

"Yes, I'm afraid it's that returned soldier I went to see. His amputation has become infected. I think it will require both of us. Are you able to come?"

"At once," Thomas agreed, reaching for his bag. He glanced at Sarah and then at Ellie. "Would you ladies be able to man the fort while we're gone? Mrs

Anderson was going to bring young Arthur in for a check-up, and there might be others, of course…"

"I would be glad to," Sarah said quickly. She looked at Ellie shyly. "Miss Phillips, would you help me? I'm still learning my way around here. Perhaps you could show me…?"

Ellie felt her throat tightening again. She looked around at the three kind, expectant faces. "I … can't," she said, her voice sounding choked. "I'm sorry, but I can't. I must get back … to Mother … and Charlie."

Feeling the all-too-familiar burning sensation behind her eyes, she cast around wildly, seized the prescription from where it hung in Thomas's hand, garbled a "thank you" and ran from the room.

Ten

Ellie sat at the kitchen table, peeling carrots for lunch. The potatoes and chicken were already sizzling in the oven. Despite the delicious smells that filled the air, she couldn't remember a bleaker Christmas morning. Even last year had been better; they hadn't heard from Father, but at least he was still alive. They still had hope.

And Jack... Ellie bit down hard on the inside of her cheek to prevent the infuriating tears from spilling at the memory of Christmas night last year, when she and Jack had sneaked down to the cliff top to exchange gifts. Missing him was a physical pain, dragging at her chest, making it hard to breathe. But even that was easier to bear than the constant worry, the relentless thoughts that rampaged through her brain – each more horrifying than the last – about what could be happening to him.

The atmosphere in church that morning had been more sober than usual, and the congregation was looking very depleted. How many of their men they had lost. There was scarcely a family left intact.

Ellie had felt a pang looking at the Mertens family, so far from home and now surrounded by battered, war-weary strangers. They were huddled together in the grey light that spilled in through the church windows, looking cold and tired. It wasn't the jolly Christmas Ellie had promised Camille and Olivier.

Charlie jolted her from her thoughts as he came tearing into the kitchen behind his new ball, squealing happily. He ran into Ellie's legs and wrapped his arms around them, laughing up at her. She couldn't help but smile back. She didn't know how he could be so unaffected by the sombre mood, but she was very grateful that he was. She dropped a kiss on to his blonde curls. He smelled of milk and wood-smoke.

"Are you having a nice time?" she asked him, enjoying the solid weight of him against her legs, the closest thing you got to a cuddle when Charlie was awake these days.

"Yes!" he declared. And then: "'Tatoes?"

Ellie laughed. "Potatoes," she agreed. "But not yet. We've got a little while to wait still. Did you eat all your toast?"

Realizing that more food was not going to be forthcoming, Charlie disentangled himself from her legs and ran off. As he raced back through the kitchen door, he collided with Aunt Frances.

"*Oof!* Easy there, Charlie boy," she wheezed, holding her soot-covered hands – dirty from building the fire in the living room – high above his clean best shirt. "Don't wake your mother," she added as he tore from the room.

She moved to the sink to wash her hands. "Well, he's full of festive spirit, anyway," she chuckled, examining her nails in the light and then returning them to the water for further scrubbing.

"At least someone is," Ellie replied, hacking savagely at a carrot.

Her aunt put an arm around her. "It's not the merriest of Christmases, is it? But still, we must make the best of it. Here, budge over and I'll tackle those turnips."

Ellie smiled as she slid her chair along to make room and handed her a knife. Thank goodness her aunt had been able to join them for Christmas; Ellie couldn't bear to think what the day would have been like without Aunt Frances's brisk cheer. Her aunt was the most inspirational woman Ellie knew. They hardly saw her because she lived in Brighton, where she worked as a nurse, and her absence had weighed all the heavier since Father's death.

They sat companionably, exchanging stories and confidences as they finished the vegetables, then put them into the oven with the chicken. Ellie revelled in Aunt Frances' accounts of Brighton, her friends and her job. In turn, her aunt chuckled over Ellie's tales of Endstone life. With Jack gone, her aunt's support was more precious than ever, and Ellie cherished this rare moment together, sharing hopes and frustrations.

"It's going to be quite a feast," said Aunt Frances, sighing contentedly as the oven door closed.

Ellie smiled, gratefully allowing herself to be enveloped by her aunt's good cheer.

Mother looked pinched and wan as they gathered round the table. She flinched at every scrape of a chair leg against the floor or a knife against a plate, and merely picked at her food. Ellie and Aunt Frances tried to keep the conversation going, but the atmosphere weighed heavily, like a thick blanket, smothering every attempt at festivity.

Mother cleared her throat. "This is all rather flavourless, Eleanor. I don't think you added enough salt to anything."

Ellie bristled, feeling her frustration bubbling up to the surface. Her mother had got up to go to church, and had returned to bed as soon as they had got home, where she had stayed until lunchtime.

"I added plenty of salt," she snapped. "Perhaps if you would let me work in the factory as I asked, we would be able to afford to pay our bill at the store and buy some better ingredients. This is the best I could do with what we have."

Mother glowered at her. "I wonder how you dare

speak to me that way. If your father were here you would see his belt, Eleanor."

It was untrue, of course. Father could certainly be strict, but he had never hit Ellie in her life. Still, it *was* true that he wouldn't have allowed her to speak to Mother like that.

Ellie swallowed hard, digging her fingernails hard into her palms. "I'm sorry, Mother. I shouldn't have spoken to you that way."

Mother looked surprised but gave a curt nod. Ellie felt Aunt Frances's hand pat her knee reassuringly under the table.

The rest of lunch passed without incident. When it was finished, Ellie and Aunt Frances cleared away the plates and then served the Christmas pudding that Ellie had made back in November. She braced herself for Mother to say how dry it was, but her mother seemed determined to be more pleasant. She nibbled delicately at her portion and didn't contradict Aunt Frances when she said it was delicious. Charlie, of course, gobbled his down with the same gusto with which he had consumed his chicken, then clamoured for more.

Ellie couldn't help smiling. Learning to cook had

been a long, slow process, and she appreciated at least one happy customer.

While they finished their puddings, Ellie asked Aunt Frances about her nursing work and soon her aunt was regaling them with a story about a young injured soldier who had sleepwalked one night and got into bed with a ward-mate. Her impersonation of the other soldier's expression when she had found them curled up together – surprised but anxious not to disturb the sleepwalker – had Ellie in fits of giggles, which in turn made Charlie laugh, even though he didn't understand the story. Mother didn't join in, but she did ask Aunt Frances more about the hospital and the other nurses.

Aunt Frances eagerly described her colleagues and the different wards she worked on. "It's such hard work, but so fabulously rewarding," she said. "I think we all know the frustrations of being stuck at home, watching our men go off and not able to *do* anything. At least this way I feel as though – every so often – I can make a positive difference."

Ellie gazed at her, rapt. As her mother glanced down to take another dainty spoonful of pudding, Aunt Frances gave her a quick wink.

"You must feel the same thing with your Women's Institute group, Josephine?" she said.

Mother's knitting circle had recently evolved to become the local branch of the Women's Institute and was now focused predominantly on producing food. Mother hadn't been going as often now she was ill, but Ellie knew that she enjoyed it. She had managed for the first time to strike up friendships with some of the other Endstone ladies. She returned from the meetings looking healthier and more enthused than Ellie had ever seen her before.

"Yes," Mother said slowly, looking warily at Aunt Frances. "I suppose I do."

"It seems like a wonderful thing to be involved in, so worthwhile. We all need to make our contribution to the war effort or we should go mad just waiting around for it to be over!" Aunt Frances laughed brightly. "And besides, we have a duty, don't you think?"

Mother stared at her, eyes narrowed. "Yes, of course, but..."

"That's why I wonder – and of course, it's none of my business – whether Ellie might be on to something with her idea of working at the factory."

Ellie inhaled. She hadn't been expecting this sudden turn in the conversation. Mother opened her mouth to protest, but Aunt Frances hurried on. "You're not well enough to work there yourself, Josephine, anyone can see that. But you seem strong enough to take care of Charlie, especially now that he's such a big boy." She smiled at her nephew and he beamed back, his face still sticky with pudding. "And Ellie tells me that there are other women in the village who would be more than happy to help out with him if it were needed."

Mother scowled at Ellie but didn't attempt to interrupt.

"Ellie is a young woman now," Aunt Frances continued. "It's right that she should do her bit for this country. And for this family." Her tone softened. "Forgive me if I'm speaking out of turn, Josephine, but with Wesley gone things must be a bit of a struggle. Why not let Ellie help out if she wants to?"

Ellie was sitting on the very edge of her seat, looking between Mother and Aunt Frances. She dared not say anything for fear of breaking the delicate spell Aunt Frances was weaving.

Finally Mother spoke. "You don't know what it's

like there," she said, so quietly that they had to lean forward to hear her. "Neither of you does." She turned to glare at Ellie. "I don't know what you imagine, Eleanor, but I assure you it's nothing like as romantic in reality."

"It's true, Mother," said Ellie gently, "I don't know what it's like. But I'm fit and healthy. It can't be right for you to work there and me to stay comfortably at home with Charlie."

She held her breath. Mother was staring at the red tablecloth – their smart one, reserved for special occasions – her dessertspoon still in her hand as though she had forgotten it was there.

"You would have to promise to let me know immediately if it was getting too much for you," Mother said at last.

Ellie felt her eyes widening. "I will, I promise," she breathed.

"I mean it, Eleanor." Mother looked up fiercely. "You'll find that people there will not be as indulgent as you're used to. You needn't expect any sympathy from them. You will come to me if you are becoming unwell or are in any danger."

Ellie bit down on the many things she could have said in response and simply nodded. Aunt Frances had fallen silent and was staring fixedly at the remains of her pudding.

"Well, then. I can see you're determined. Just don't complain when you find it isn't all adventure and excitement. When I think of the fuss you used to make about going to school..."

"I won't," Ellie replied, a little louder this time. "Oh, Mother, thank you! I will work so hard there, and everything will get better for us. You'll see."

Her mother grunted but said no more. Ellie seized Aunt Frances's hand under the table and squeezed it tight. She meant every word she had said. This was her chance; at last, her chance to improve things for her family ... and for herself.

Eleven

Ellie was already waiting on the dark platform when the train pulled into Endstone station. She was soon joined by many others – men and women – rushing in from all directions. She had taken the train only a handful of times in her life and she loved everything about it: the billowing steam, the shrill conductor's whistle, the green doors that opened and closed with a satisfying *clunk*.

Ellie climbed carefully aboard, her lunch pail banging against her leg. She settled into a seat by the window, ignoring the grumblings of the other passengers as they clambered past each other into the carriage. Finally everyone was aboard. The last few doors slammed shut, the conductor blew his whistle and the train lurched into motion.

The other passengers, accustomed to the journey, nestled back into their seats at once, leaning against windows or each other, and closed their eyes. It was early – far earlier than Ellie usually got up – but she was too excited – and nervous – to sleep. Instead, she peered out into the dark countryside as the train rattled along, squinting to make out farms and houses, roads and the winding river. Her breath misted the glass so that she had to keep wiping it clear with her scarf.

Eventually she turned her attention to her sleeping companions. Although these were Endstone people, their faces were not familiar. Most of the factory workers lived on the other side of the village, like Jack's family, and Mother didn't like Ellie to go there. Many of them she had probably passed in the store or at church, but their faces had not stuck; their worlds had always been so separate.

Until now.

After only half an hour, the train chugged to a halt at the station nearest to the factory. Ellie felt her stomach give a corresponding heave. The other men and women in the carriage were already on their feet and Ellie fumbled with the door, feeling their impatience as they shuffled behind her. She hopped down on to the platform and was swiftly overtaken by the crowd.

Looking around her, she was staggered by the number of people pouring off the train and on to the road that led towards the factory. She thought of Jack, who had been coming here for years. She had tried so many times to imagine what it would be like, what his days involved, so different from her own – and now here she was, seeing it for herself.

Jack would not have believed his eyes!

Now that she was here in this place she associated so strongly with him, he felt closer than ever. She could almost see him, bounding along the road, laughing and jostling with some of the other young boys; she could imagine his voice booming above their murmured conversation. She bit down so hard on her bottom lip that she could taste blood. She shouldn't be thinking about Jack, she told herself crossly. She was here to work.

Glancing to one side, she saw a young woman with a grey skirt and tired eyes shuffling beside her.

"Hello," Ellie said timidly. "My name's Ellie. This is

my first day working here."

The woman's eyes widened ever so slightly. "Marie," she grunted.

"Have you worked at the factory for long?" Ellie cringed at how posh and formal her voice sounded.

"For ever, feels like. Ever since school." Marie's voice was slow, reluctant.

"Do you like it?" Again, Ellie felt herself flinch. The woman's eyebrows raised and her lip curled imperceptibly.

"Ooh, yes," she drawled. "It's a chuckle a minute in there."

Ellie gave an apologetic laugh. Marie did not join in. "I suppose ... I suppose I thought it might be a bit more exciting now you're ... now we're part of the war effort?"

Marie no longer bothered to even attempt to disguise her look of disdain. "Take it from me, girly, it doesn't make a blind bit of difference *what* you're making – it's all the same work. Only change is now we have to work longer hours than ever, with less men. And daft kids like you come along and treat it like a jolly day out."

108

Before Ellie could gather herself to respond, Marie had stomped off to join another group of women up ahead. Ellie watched her go, her face burning.

Stupid, stupid, she thought furiously to herself, pressing the back of her hand to her hot cheeks.

The factory loomed ominously ahead. Still replaying the humiliating conversation in her head, she joined the long queue of women pouring through the door. The men had peeled off and were entering a separate section of the factory. For the first time, Ellie realized that Jack's father would be among them.

At the front of the queue was a desk where the women were signing their names before heading off to a large cloakroom area. Ellie croaked her name to the impatient-looking man behind the register, her throat dry, and presented her letter from the factory manager in which he had agreed to take her on in Mother's stead. After a cursory glance, the man brushed the letter aside and pointed her in the direction of a store cupboard, instructing her to collect some overalls, leave her own clothes on a peg in the cloakroom, and tie her hair back before reporting back to receive her instructions.

Ellie pulled on the large, grey overalls with shaking hands. The material was stiff and hung off her in heavy folds. All around were large signs reminding the workers that cigarettes, matches or anything else that could cause a spark were strictly prohibited on the premises.

When she arrived back at the desk, the man didn't even look up. Instead a freckle-faced girl, about her own age, was waiting for her.

"Hello, I'm Daisy. Ellie, is it? I'm to show you around. Come on."

Ellie was only too happy to leave the stony-faced clerk behind and follow Daisy, who kept up a steady stream of chatter. Ellie could barely keep up, she was so distracted by the clanging, crashing sounds and strange smells all around her. Luckily Daisy didn't seem to expect a reply

"Here, pop this cap on," she said, as they reached a cavernous room, filled with orderly rows of women, all setting up at their work stations. The room was lined with shelves of shining metal canisters.

Ellie took the grey cap, which matched the one perched on top of Daisy's sandy hair, and followed her to an empty space on one of the rows.

"You can work here beside me," Daisy said. "Now, watch."

Ellie obediently trained her eyes on the work station.

"We take the empty shell cases from this section – see? Then you use your funnel – here's a spare one for you – and scoop the powder from those sacks into the shell. Use a broom –" Daisy brandished one to demonstrate "– to tamp it down. Then add more powder, tamp it down, add more, and so on until the shell is full. All right? Then once it's completely full up, carry it over to that area there. Blooming heavy when they're full, mind. But just be careful you don't drop one or we'll all be blown sky high!" She laughed.

Ellie winced then nodded. It seemed simple enough, and she was glad to have something practical to throw herself into. Everyone else seemed to know each other, and she felt conspicuous in her newness.

As she began to work – scooping, pouring and tamping – Daisy continue to babble away, telling her in hushed tones about the other women who worked here, the two foremen, along with stories that her younger brothers had reported from the men's section.

When Ellie's first shell was filled – Daisy had filled three in this time – she put her funnel down and went to lift it. It wouldn't move at all at the first attempt.

"Told you it was heavy," Daisy laughed. "Bend your knees and wrap your arms around it – helps to get a bit more of a handle on it."

Ellie did as instructed. Every muscle in her arms, back and shoulders strained and heaved. Each step cost her an enormous effort; it felt like ten full minutes before she had travelled the same number of metres. As she finally lowered the shell – with a clang that made her wince – she released the breath she hadn't realized she was holding, and noticed with shame that her arms were shaking.

"You'll get used to it," Daisy said sympathetically as Ellie rejoined her. "You'd be surprised how quick you build up the muscle." She demonstrated a bulging bicep in an otherwise scrawny arm, then leaned over and gave Ellie a surreptitious pat on the shoulder. "Sorry, I'd have helped you if I could, only the foreman gets cross if he thinks we're wasting time. Don't want my wages docked."

Ellie got back to work filling her next shell. Her dread of having to lift it made her want to go slowly, but she was equally afraid the foreman would think she was slacking. She shovelled the powder through the funnel as quickly as she could without spilling it.

When her next shell was filled, she gritted her teeth and heaved it up into her arms. And she had thought Charlie was heavy! Waddling ungracefully over to the appointed area, she found herself moving alongside an older woman, who carried her own shell with enviable ease.

"Daisy says you're Josephine Phillips' daughter," she said, smiling. Clamping her shell against her chest with one hand – after glancing briefly around – she used her other hand to support one of Ellie's trembling elbows.

"Yes," Ellie puffed, managing a small but grateful smile back. "I'm Ellie."

"Ida Stokes," the other woman said, as they progressed painfully forwards. "You don't look much like your mum, do you?"

Ellie's kept her arms wrapped tightly around the shell as she shook her head. It was true; Ellie looked a lot more like Father, something she'd always been glad of, however beautiful her mother might be.

"How's she doing? Any better? We were worried about her when she didn't come back. Although I can't say as we were surprised. Not really cut out for this sort of work, is she?"

Ellie nodded in agreement, trying to ignore the nagging thought that she might not be cut out for it herself.

"You tell her we were asking for her, won't you?" said another woman, helping Ellie to lower her shell to the ground among the others. "I'm Edith," she added, with a broad grin, which revealed a gap between her front teeth.

Ellie smiled back, wiping her hands, which were slick with sweat, on her overalls.

As the women walked back together, yet another – who looked to be in her mid-twenties – fell into step beside them. "I just hope you don't give yourself the same airs and graces she did," she said. "There's no place for them here."

"You be quiet, Helen Fredericks," said Edith sharply. "Leave the girl alone; it's only her first day."

"We've all got work to do," sniffed Helen. "We can't be carrying the likes of her. Everyone must be able to take care of themselves."

Ellie kept her eyes low, feeling her aching fists clench, but before she could summon a response, Ida had rejoined with: "And some of us remember your first day all too well, Helen. Didn't I find you crying in the lavs in the first hour, and have to drag you out before the foreman realized and sent you packing?"

There was a burst of laughter from some of the nearby women, and Helen stalked off, her neck flushed.

As Ellie drew the next empty shell towards her, she found the corners of her mouth turning up despite her muscles feeling as though they'd been run over repeatedly with a tractor. Daisy caught her eye and winked back.

The day wore on, with a short break for lunch, during which Ellie barely had the energy to lift her sandwich to her mouth. Most of the women kept up cheerful conversation, and Ellie was grateful for it; it helped to give her a focus beyond her aching body.

Back on the factory floor, the repetitiveness of the work – when not hauling shells – was hypnotic. More than once she found herself drifting off in an exhausted haze, and missing questions directed at her by the others.

On one such occasion, she caught herself replaying her conversation with unfriendly Marie from that morning. "Exciting" she had called the work. Her brow furrowed. It felt purposeful, that was for sure; important. But it didn't do to think too hard about what it was that she was helping to produce; to picture the shells landing and blowing apart earth, trees, buildings, bodies...

The funnel slipped from her fingers and she had to chase it as it rolled across the floor. A chorus of friendly laughter went up around her.

Don't think like that, Ellie told herself angrily as she ran to catch the funnel. *What good does it do? Someone else would be doing the work if I wasn't. And we need the money.*

Finally the end of the day arrived. Ellie felt as though she had scarcely had a moment to draw breath since the morning; yet she could have sworn she was ten years older than she had been when she had stepped off the train.

As she queued to splash her face at the sink in the cloakroom – it was as if the powder was encrusting every inch of her, even her eyeballs – she tried and failed to imagine Mother here. Ellie had always thought of herself as strong and hardy, but right now she wanted nothing more than to drop to her knees and sleep where she landed. How had her delicate mother lasted five minutes here, let alone all those weeks that she had returned, day after day?

Ellie peeled off her overalls and cap and put them on to her peg, too tired even to be shy of the other women changing around her. She didn't understand how they could be so loud and jovial; she could barely speak without slurring her words. Their voices reverberated in her head...

"Come on, slowcoach," Daisy chided, finding her leaning against the wall, one leg into her skirt, with no idea how long she'd been standing there. "We'll miss the train at this rate."

The thought of having to wait any longer before she could crawl into her bed managed to inspire Ellie to a burst of speed. She fumbled with the buttons on her jacket, then hurried out behind Daisy.

The walk to the station felt twice as long as it had in the morning. Daisy seemed finally to have realized that she wasn't going to get much conversation out of Ellie and was chattering away to another girl, leaving Ellie to plod slowly behind them, gazing blearily ahead. The boys and men were pouring out of their part of the factory to mingle with the women and create one large, jostling crowd.

Yet again, she found her mind wandering back to Jack... No wonder he was always so hungry, if the work was this hard, she thought to herself. She didn't understand how he'd had the energy to come and visit her, or to meet in the woods or at the beach after work, as they had so often done. She longed to speak to him, to compare stories.

She shook her head briskly. This was silly. Thinking about Jack was causing her mind to play tricks. She was even beginning to imagine that she could see him... One particular boy in the group of young men ahead of her looked just like him; about the same height and build, with the same brown hair curling out from beneath his cap and on to his freckled neck...

She looked away, shaking her head, but found her gaze drawn back only moments later.

The boy turned to his companion to say something

and Ellie stopped short, feeling her heart give one deep *thud* against her ribs before seeming to halt completely.

Jack?

Jack!

"Jack!" Her voice was hoarse. The cry that emerged sounded like a crow's call.

Twelve

The boy didn't turn. He was surrounded by four or five boys of about his age, nodding to what one of them was saying. He hadn't heard her.

Ellie forgot her tiredness. She ran, pushing past people to catch up with him, her lunch pail clanging and her skirt whipping around her legs, threatening to trip her. She lurched through the group of boys to grab his elbow, causing grumbles of "Steady now!" and "Watch where you're going!".

At last he turned and, stumbling to a halt, Ellie drank in the sight of her friend.

"Jack!"

It was as though she had imagined him into being.

She'd thought and thought and thought about him,

and here he was. A grin spread across her face and she tightened her grip on his arm.

It was really him!

"What are you doing here?" he asked her.

"What am *I* doing here?" she exploded. "What am I—?" She drew a breath. "I *work* here now. Oh, but never mind that. What about *you*? I thought you were in France! You were... I thought... Oh, Jack!"

She couldn't help herself; she flung herself into his arms, breathing in his smell, wrapping her arms so tightly around him that she reawoke all her stiff, complaining muscles.

Everything would be all right now. Everything would be fine. She wouldn't have to do it all on her own any more.

Somebody whistled. A few laughs went up. The crowd continued to flow around them like a stream around a boulder, but Ellie ignored it all. It took her a long moment to realize that Jack's arms had remained at his side, his posture rigid. Something dark and sickly seemed to trickle down her throat and pool in her stomach; she felt her lips fall. She opened her eyes, his dark green jacket blurring in her near vision.

Slowly, so slowly, she released him and took a half-step away.

His cheeks were pink, but his expression was cold, his jaw tensed. His eyes seemed to skim the top of her head.

"Why ... why didn't you let me know you were back?" she asked, her voice quieter now.

He shrugged but didn't say anything.

"When did you get home?" She found that she was dreading the answer.

"Couple of days ago." His voice sounded so different, so flat, no trace of the booming laughter that had always been on the verge of bursting out of him.

"And ... *why*?" Ellie had a horrible feeling she was sounding like Mother when she was in interrogation mode.

Jack made an impatient sound in the back of his throat. "Military inspection. They realized my papers were fake and sent me back as soon as they could."

He wouldn't even look at her. She wanted to shake him. "Jack! Talk to me! What was it like? Don't shrug!" She heard her voice getting more shrill, felt people looking at her, but she couldn't stop. "I can't believe you didn't tell me you were going! I can't believe you didn't tell me you were back! Why are you being like this?"

When at last his eyes lowered to meet hers – he had grown again, she realized – they were dull, lifeless, just like his voice.

"Calm down, Ellie, I don't know why you're getting yourself into such a flap. I was going to come and see you soon. I've just been busy since I got back."

She opened her mouth but then closed it again. *Busy?* When had Jack ever been too busy to see her before?

"Look," he went on, glancing about, "we'll miss the train if you carry on, and it's not the time to go into any of this. I'm going to catch up with the lads, but we can speak later. All right?"

She just looked at him. He jogged off without waiting for a response. She watched him go, rooted to the ground, buffeted by the bodies still surging past her. He rejoined the group of boys. One of them glanced in her direction, then leaned in to say something to him. He didn't look back.

Ellie used the end of her scarf to angrily scrub the

hot tears from her eyes before they had a chance to spill down her cheeks.

What had happened? He hadn't missed her at all, wasn't in the least pleased to see her.

She had been thinking about him all this time, and wishing, wishing, wishing him safe and home; and here he was – but it was as though he were a completely different person, as though he'd left her friend Jack behind in France and someone else had come along in his body. He hadn't even asked how she was, didn't seem to care that she was working in the factory, or what that might mean.

Had she done something to upset him, to make him be so cold and uncaring? What could it possibly be? But she hadn't had a chance to upset him...

Daisy reappeared at her side. "There you are! Hurry up, dreamer; now we have to run. Ooh, are you all right? You're not crying, are you?"

"Course not." Ellie gave a great sniff, thinking with grim satisfaction how horrified Mother would be to hear it. "I think it's the powder, making my eyes sore."

"Oh, yes, it does that. But you'll get used to it. Come on!"

They ran, clinging on to each other's hands, all the way to the platform and on to the waiting train. It was dark already and as the train's motion became more rhythmic, Daisy's chatter stopped for the first time all day and her head slumped against Ellie's shoulder. Within moments, she was emitting little snores.

Ellie looked at her wan reflection in the window; her eyes appeared bigger and darker than usual, her eyebrows drawn together and her mouth set in a straight line. *Now I look like Mother*, she thought.

Then, before she could stop herself, her mind strayed back to Jack; where on the train he might be sitting, what he was thinking about, whether he'd wait for her when they arrived at Endstone... *That's enough,* she told herself. *Jack Scott has had enough of my thoughts and my time and my worry. I will waste no more on him.*

If only she could follow her own instructions.

Thirteen

Ellie woke early as usual, staring into the dark of the bedroom and steeling herself to push back the blankets and brave the cold morning air. Just as she was about to give herself a countdown, she remembered: it was Saturday; she could go back to sleep.

With a happy sigh, she snuggled deeper under the covers and was asleep again in moments.

When she next awoke, it was getting light; she could see cold sunlight spilling round the edges of the heavy curtain. She lay for a moment, making minute, experimental movements with her limbs and wincing as the pain rippled all over her body. She had been working at the factory for over a month now and Daisy had been right: she was getting used to the work; her body was getting stronger. The muscles in her arms, legs and back were hard, her hands were calloused, and she was now able to lift the full shells without needing help. But the bone-deep tiredness, the aching in her limbs, didn't seem to get any easier to bear. Nor was she any more used to the feeling that the powder had insinuated itself into every nook and cranny of her body. She never felt clean no matter how thoroughly she washed.

She sighed again, preparing herself to get up. Day off or not, Mother would be bound to comment if she slept too late.

Then she remembered something which caused her to slump back against the pillow once more. Today was her birthday. She was fifteen.

Before she could stop them, memories of her fourteenth birthday came crashing in like waves against the cliff face. The news about Father had been so recent. Mother hadn't even got out of bed, and she and Charlie had had a sad meal of soup. Jack had come round though. He had bought her a book as a gift – one that the school teacher Miss Smith had advised him Ellie would like. Glancing over at her bookshelf, Ellie could see its red spine jutting out.

She scowled and pulled the pillow over her head. She didn't want to think about Jack, or the fact that he was her only happy memory from her last birthday. She had barely seen him since that first day at the factory; the promised conversation had never taken place and she was far too angry with him to do anything about it herself.

"Eleanor! Ellie!" Mother's voice floated up the stairs.

Ellie?

She thrust the pillow to one side and sat up. Things had been much better with Mother lately. The time apart was doing them both good, as was the easing of the financial pressures that came from Ellie working. She felt a joyful glowing in her chest when she presented Mother with her wages every week...

Still, Mother *never* called her Ellie.

And it wouldn't do to risk her good humour by making her wait.

"Coming!" she called back, pushing back the blankets and leaping out of bed. She hurriedly tore off her nightdress and pulled on a skirt, stockings, blouse and cardigan. Splashing her face and mouth at the basin on the dressing table, she cast a critical eye at her reflection. She quickly pulled a brush through her dark, tangled hair and tied it back with a ribbon.

Then she clattered down the stairs and into the kitchen. She saw her mother wince at the noise, but manage a smile nonetheless.

"Good morning, Eleanor." She leant over to give Ellie a cool kiss on the cheek. "And happy birthday."

"Thank you, Mother," Ellie said, feeling strangely shy. "Good morning to you too."

"Charlie," Mother said, smoothing his curls. "Are you going to say happy birthday to your sister?"

He blinked at her.

"Say, 'Happy birthday, Eleanor'," she pronounced carefully.

"Ha birdy, Lellie."

Ellie laughed and scooped him up into her arms with an *oof* – he was getting so heavy now. "Thank you, Charlie."

"Sit down," Mother was saying to her now. "Have some breakfast."

The sight of the boiled egg, toast, teapot and the envelope with *Eleanor* written in Mother's elegant hand leaning against it almost brought tears to Ellie's eyes. She sat down before her mother could notice, depositing Charlie in the chair next to her.

Ellie watched as Mother poured the tea. She was looking so much better at last. She had always been pale, but the sickly shade of the past months had been replaced by her usual clear, smooth skin. She was eating more, Ellie noted, and her bones were less prominent.

"I thought it would be nice to have a bit of a birthday tea for you this afternoon," Mother said.

Ellie looked at her. Mother volunteering to do something frivolous?

"That would be lovely," she said carefully, not taking her eyes from her mother's face.

"It has been a while since we've had anything to celebrate," Mother went on slowly, while buttering her toast. Her face was perfectly calm. "You and I could make a cake, if you liked."

"Cake!" Charlie declared before Ellie could answer. "Cake, cake!"

130

Ellie and Mother looked at each other and laughed.

"I thought we could invite Thomas and perhaps those Belgian children." Ellie lowered her spoon and gazed with naked surprise at her mother. "And the Scotts. Jack's back, I understand. We could ask him and his sister. You'd like that, wouldn't you?"

"The *Scotts*?" Mother had never made any bones of her disapproval of Ellie's friendship with Jack, and *now* she was offering to have him round for tea and cake!

"Well, yes, Eleanor. I really don't know why you're looking at me like that. You've been moping around for weeks, I thought you would be pleased."

Ellie made a face. Now this sounded more like Mother.

"You've been working hard; you deserve to have a nice birthday."

Ellie's eyes swam.

"And ... I'm sure your father would have suggested the same thing, were he here."

Ellie gave a subtle sniff but smiled. "Oh, yes, he always loved a tea party!"

"Especially if there were the possibility of a sing-song around the piano afterwards."

They laughed again. Father's singing talents had not quite matched his enthusiasm.

They finished breakfast and tidied the things away together. Then they started work on a Victoria sponge cake. Ellie pulled a chair up to the counter so that Charlie could "help", and Mother didn't even protest when he got batter all over himself.

When the cake was in the oven, she said, "Well, hadn't you better run out and invite your guests?"

"Oh, yes," said Ellie, feeling an unfamiliar smile on her face. "I'll go to the surgery and call in to the Mertens on the way."

"And the Scotts," Mother went on. "You could drop into the shop and ask Anna."

Ellie's smile faltered somewhat. "Yes, of course," she said slowly.

"Run along, then."

Ellie washed up the last of the batter-smeared spoons and bowls, cleaned her hands and took off her apron. She grabbed Charlie as he raced past and wiped the jam from around his mouth as he protested and squirmed. When she caught Mother looking at her, she realized she had run out of excuses. Pulling on her coat, she shuffled out of the front door.

She took her bicycle and peddled carefully down the steep and frosty slope to the path that ran behind the village square. The winter berries in the hedgerows were as bright as splashes of blood; a robin kept pace with her as she cycled, darting along from branch to branch.

She called into the surgery first. Thomas was out on call and Dr Mertens was with a patient. Sarah was helping out in the waiting room again. She seemed delighted to be invited to tea, but told Ellie she could not be spared from the surgery. She wished her a happy birthday so warmly that it made the younger girl blush. Sarah urged her to ask Camille and Olivier; she was sure they would love to go.

The Mertens lived in a small cottage only minutes away, in the direction of the station. It had been empty since the previous owners – an elderly couple – had died; their children had long since grown up and moved away.

Ellie had never been inside the cottage; she hesitated in front of its freshly painted forget-me-not-blue door, with its trailing fringe of ivy. At last she lifted the knocker and rapped smartly. There was no answer, though she could hear cheerful voices not far away. After knocking again, she paused to listen.

The voices were coming from outside.

Walking round to the side of the house, she saw a tall gate that was slightly ajar. As she moved closer the voices got louder.

"Hello," she called, knocking on the gate. She pushed it open and walked along a small pathway with an evergreen bush arching over it. Finally she emerged into an overgrown garden.

In the centre, knee-deep in weeds and fallen leaves, were Camille and Olivier Mertens. Their coats were unbuttoned and their cheeks flushed; beside them lay a pile of discarded hats, gloves and scarves. They seemed to be arranging bricks and rotting planks of wood into some sort of structure.

"Hello," Ellie said again, quietly, causing them to break off their heated conversation – of which she couldn't understand a word.

"Ellie!" exclaimed Camille, her cheeks turning an even darker shade of red. "Hello! I am sorry – we

134

didn't see you there."

"That's all right, I haven't been here long. What . . . what are you doing?"

"We are making a fort!" Olivier declared proudly. His sister swatted him with her hand. "What?" he demanded.

"Well," Ellie said, "it looks good." She envied them the activity. It struck her as exactly the sort of thing she and Jack would have loved to do when they were younger. When things were different.

"I was wondering. . ." she went on. "You see, it's my birthday and we're having tea and cake later. I . . . we wondered if you would like to join us?"

Camille's cheeks flushed again, but her smile was broad. "Happy birthday! We would love to come to tea."

"Many happy returns," Olivier added solemnly.

"Oh, good," Ellie said, feeling an answering smile spread across her face. "Four o' clock all right for you?"

"That sounds perfect," Camille said.

Ellie was still smiling as she retrieved her bicycle from the front of the cottage. Then she remembered that the most challenging part of her task was still ahead.

Somehow, though, despite Jack's coldness since he had returned, she couldn't imagine him turning down an invitation for tea and cake – an invitation that had originated with her mother, no less.

She found herself grinning at the thought of his surprise.

And it was her birthday, after all!

Suddenly she felt sure that Jack had only needed the right opportunity to return to his old self. Maybe he'd had a bad time out in France. It must have been hard for him to have been sent back with his tail between his legs after he'd been talking about going for so long. She began to speed up. She should have been more patient with him. Why did she always have to be so stubborn? She imagined how Jack would have been if she had been the one behaving out of sorts. He wouldn't have given up on her; he'd have badgered her and badgered her until she told him what was wrong.

She skidded to a halt outside the shop and leaned her bicycle against the window. She was relieved, despite her new resolve, to see that Anna was alone.

The girls greeted each other warmly – Anna, never

one to bear a grudge, hadn't mentioned the late grocery bill since it had been paid – and Ellie extended her invitation.

Anna brightened visibly. "That would be great! Can't remember when I was last invited to a tea party! I'll be closing up here shortly, and can head up then."

"Wonderful," Ellie said. She dropped her gaze to the counter, staring intently at the jars of coffee and tea leaves. "Do you think Jack might come too?"

The pause was long enough to fill her with doubt. Anna's expression was unreadable. But she simply said: "Course. Never known our Jack say no to cake, have you?"

"No," Ellie agreed, knowing that Anna must have noticed her relief. "I'll see you soon then."

She raced home as fast as she could to help Mother make sandwiches and to get changed. Mother's birthday gift to her had been one of her own dresses, adjusted so that it would fit Ellie. It was by far the most grown-up dress she had ever owned. A soft grey colour, it suited Mother's pale tones more than it did Ellie's, but she had been touched to note the addition of pale blue ribbon around the hem, collar and sleeves. Brushing her thick hair and tying it back with a matching blue ribbon, Ellie surveyed herself critically in the mirror. Smoothing down the front of the dress, she returned downstairs just as a knock at the door signified the arrival of the Mertens.

Soon Ellie was busy. Mother had laid the table in the sitting room, and Ellie poured tea and passed around sandwiches and cake. She was busy preventing Charlie from getting his sticky fingers all over Camille's pretty skirt when Mother opened the door to Jack and Anna.

Ellie could feel Jack's eyes on her as he walked in. She straightened and turned with a smile, but he had moved straight to the window and was looking out into the back garden. He didn't turn around.

Ellie was immediately greeted by Anna, who handed her a loaf of her mother's fruitcake. With relief, Ellie carried it to the kitchen so that she could slice it.

Back in the sitting room, the atmosphere was tense. It took Ellie a moment to realize why. While

Charlie was burbling happily to Anna and Olivier, and Camille was speaking politely with Mother, Jack was brooding silently in the corner, away from everyone else. Ellie was sure she was not the only one who was aware of it.

She moved towards him to offer him tea. Jack declined politely yet curtly. Ellie had barely had time to think what to say next, when Charlie, who until now hadn't realized Jack was here, gave a joyful shout.

"Jack!"

Seizing one of his toy soldiers, he toddled over to the window and tugged on Jack's sleeve. "Play, Jack? Darden?"

"Not now, Charlie," Jack said, his voice flat. He dropped his hand as though to tousle the little boy's hair, but his fingers barely made contact. "Excuse me," he said abruptly and stalked out of the room.

Ellie stared after him, astonished. Jack had always had endless patience with Charlie.

There was a moment's pause, and then Anna made a sound of exasperation. "Oh, for goodness's sake!" she exploded, causing Mother to wince. "I don't know what's got into him, but I've had just about enough! He's been like this all the time since he came home. Sometimes I wish he hadn't bothered!"

"Don't say that," Ellie said, her voice barely above a whisper.

"No ... well," Anna huffed. "Well ... perhaps not. But I don't like this new Jack. You should try living with him! I'm ashamed of him, really I am."

"I think," came Jack's voice from the doorway, causing Ellie to startle and Anna to shift uncomfortably, "it would be much easier for you all to talk about me if I just left. Especially Anna," he continued loudly over Ellie's protestations, "since she's so ashamed of me. Thank you," he said stiffly in Mother's direction. "Good afternoon."

Ellie chased him down the hallway to the front door.

"Jack!"

"No, Ellie, you should go back to your guests. No one wants me here."

He stormed out of the front door and flung himself on to his bicycle.

"Jack!"

Now Anna barged past her. "God save us!" she exclaimed. "Terribly sorry, Ellie, I expect that's the last time your mam will have us round! Thanks for the nice tea. Happy birthday." And she was gone, chasing her brother down the path and muttering darkly until she was out of earshot.

Ellie gazed after them, a sharp pain between her eyebrows. She pushed the door closed and returned to the sitting room. All she wanted now was to crawl into her bed and pull the blankets over her head.

Mother said nothing, but she didn't need to; her expression was deafening. Anna was correct; the Scotts would not be invited back. Mother would for ever feel she had been right about them.

Ellie sat down and retrieved her plate. She took a mouthful of cake, to avoid having to talk, but it felt like paper in her mouth.

She glanced around the room. Olivier was playing with Charlie and the toy soldiers; Camille was still struggling to keep the conversation going with Mother, but it was clear the party was over. A little while later, Mother offered to package up some cake for the Mertens to take home to their family; they correctly read this as a hint that it was time to go, and their relief was palpable. Charlie was the only one who didn't seem pleased when the front door closed behind them.

That evening, once Charlie was asleep, Ellie sat on her bed, a sheet of paper on her lap and a pen gripped between her teeth. She had been rolling the idea of writing to Albert Murphy round in her head since they had first received his letter. So far she had always found an excuse not to, but tonight, wishing more than ever that it could be Father she was writing to, she decided the time had come.

She carefully printed the address and date at the top and then paused again.

Dear Mr Murphy, she wrote at last:
I am Wesley Phillips' daughter Eleanor – Ellie.
My mother and I were very grateful to receive your letter. Thank you so much for taking the time to write to us.
We were very sorry to hear of your injuries and wish you a full recovery.

She broke off to chew her pen, swallowing hard against the wave of emotion.

We miss my father very much, every day. Your letter and your stories helped to make him feel a little closer. I would love to hear any more you might remember, if you would not mind terribly.
Yours sincerely,
Ellie Phillips

Ellie waited for the ink to dry, then carefully folded the letter and placed it in an envelope, which she put on top of the chest by her bed. Crossing the room to her wardrobe, she took out the little wooden box that contained the half-written letter Father had never sent and, sitting on top of it, the painted shell Jack had given her the Christmas before last. Taking out the letter, the shell tumbled to the bottom of the box. She did not retrieve it, but closed the lid and put the letter under her pillow, one hand resting on top of it.

Then she reached over and turned off the light.

Fourteen

"Wakey, wakey."

Daisy's gentle shaking roused Ellie from her sleep. She lifted her head from the other girl's shoulder and wiped her mouth. She could taste the TNT and the other chemicals they used at the factory. Nowadays she could never escape them.

She rubbed her gritty eyes and looked around her. Bright sunlight was pouring into the carriage, filtered through the grimy windows. The train was rattling into Endstone station. Her fellow workers were stirring and gathering their belongings, ready to disembark.

They had been on the early shift; it was late afternoon now. The girls clambered down from the train and Ellie felt the now-familiar stiffness and aching in her joints and muscles. June was hot and that made the factory even less pleasant. Ellie spent the days dripping with sweat and, once back on the train at the end of a shift, fell into a sleep so deep it was as though she had been drugged. She took a swig from her canteen of water, longing to tip the whole thing over her head.

"Cheer up." Daisy elbowed her. "It's a beautiful evening!"

Ellie managed a smile. She didn't know why Daisy put up with her; she was hardly good company. Glad though she was to be earning money – and to escape from the house – she was finding the work as dull as it was exhausting now that the novelty had worn off. Worst of all, the repetitive nature of it gave her no break from her thoughts.

"Beautiful," she agreed, giving Daisy a small nudge back. "Enjoy it."

"Ha, chance would be a fine thing!"

The girls waved to each other and Daisy headed off to the far side of the village, where she lived with her large family. Ellie knew a whole evening of chores awaited her. As Ellie watched her go, her eyes drifted in the direction of the woods. They looked almost blue in the hazy air. She thought longingly of the summer evenings when she would meet Jack from his train after work and they would head off into the shade of the trees to talk or pick fruit, fish or paddle in the river. She imagined slipping her swollen feet into that icy water, splashing some at Jack as he lounged on the bank, drowsing with his hat over his eyes or singing a rude song he had learned from his friends at the factory.

She shook the thoughts from her head. She hadn't seen Jack in weeks. Sometimes it came as a surprise to remember that he was not still in France. According to his mother, he was working overnight shifts at the factory now, and sleeping throughout the day. Ellie still saw some of his friends around the village – those who were not old enough to have been sent away with the army – but Jack was never among them. Mabel was beside herself with worry. She had confided in Ellie that she was becoming concerned he would wind up the same way as his father.

Ellie sighed. She felt sorry for the Scotts, of course – they had been through so much – but, if she was honest, she was relieved that she wasn't the only one receiving this cold treatment from Jack.

Not that it made it any easier to know what to do about it.

Drifting along the dappled path in the direction of home, Ellie found herself at the surgery and decided to go in. She had taken to doing this more and more on her days off, or after an early shift in the factory. With all the returning wounded soldiers, not to mention the increased number of injuries among the factory workers, and the lack of food endured by the villagers, Dr Mertens and Thomas were more stretched than ever. She could see how much they were coming to rely on Sarah to keep things running when they were both out on call, and she found she liked to help whenever she could. It was a good counter-balance to the mindless dreariness of work at the factory.

Seeing her interest, Dr Mertens had begun giving her tasks that demanded more skill than simply ordering the files and taking messages. Lately he had shown her how to perform basic first aid, including bandaging wounds and changing dressings.

Ellie had warmed considerably to this kind, good-humoured doctor, and regretted the ill-feeling that she had nurtured for so long. He was – as both Jack and Thomas had told her all those months ago – a godsend to the village. She had come to value his kindness and skill as much as the other villagers.

Pushing the door open, she saw that the waiting room was full. For once, Sarah was nowhere to be seen. Ellie greeted the patients, before going to the bathroom to wash her hands and face.

When she returned, she checked the desk; sure enough, there was the appointment book and, on top, a list of the walk-in appointments written in Sarah's neat hand, names struck through once they had been seen. Thomas, she saw, was with a patient. Dr Mertens must be out on call. Checking the list, she did a lap of the room, adding the names that were not yet on it and asking whether there was anything she could do while they were waiting.

She had to smother a smile at the sight of old Miss Webb, who, she thought to herself, probably spent more time at the surgery than either of the doctors.

"Well, Eleanor, here I am again."

"Here you are," Ellie agreed, trying to keep her tone sympathetic. "How are you today, Miss Webb?"

She knew the question was a mistake as soon as it had escaped from her mouth.

"Oh, not well. Not well at all, Eleanor. If it's not my aching knees and ankles, it's my heart. If it's not my heart, it's my pounding head. I can scarcely sleep and I rarely manage to eat anything. I'm sure it's this war that's the problem. I keep expecting to be killed in my bed! Is it any wonder I can't sleep?"

Ellie made what she hoped were appropriately soothing sounds.

"And it's nigh on impossible to see a doctor these days," Miss Webb went on in an accusatory tone. She glowered round at the other patients in the room, at least two of whom were returned soldiers. Ellie followed her gaze and noticed how young they were. One had lost a leg. The other had no visible injury, but he stared blandly into space out of shaded eyes. It was these younger soldiers whose injuries – to say nothing of their loss – that the villagers found hardest to bear.

"I should hardly be having to drag myself down here at my age," Miss Webb continued. "I really would have expected a doctor to see me at home."

"No," Ellie said soothingly. "But I suppose we're all having to make sacrifices."

"Humph." Miss Webb lowered her voice but it still sounded horribly loud to Ellie. "I wish *they'd* stop at home, in any case. It gives me the jitters to look at them."

"Miss Webb!" Ellie couldn't help herself now. The older woman shuffled and muttered in her seat but her complaining subsided. "Is there anything I can help with, while you're waiting?"

"You?" Miss Webb sniffed. "I shouldn't think so, dear. I need to be seen by a doctor. I'm a complex case, as Dr Pritchard always says."

Ellie didn't trust herself to respond.

"Working at the factory now, aren't you?" Miss Webb continued.

Ellie nodded.

"Doesn't seem right, a young girl like you. Goodness knows how you're expected to find a husband. Though, I suppose with all the young men off at war…" She sighed. "What would your father have made of it, I wonder?"

Ellie bristled, but before she had time to reply, Miss

Webb went on, springing jarringly to a new topic. "Still, I suppose you've heard the news."

Ellie looked at her blankly, still thinking about Father.

"Surely you've heard?" Miss Webb insisted. "Everyone's talking about it."

"Miss Webb..." Ellie began warningly.

"About Dr Pritchard and that young Belgian girl..." Seeing Ellie's expression, she continued. "Well, they're getting married, aren't they? Next Saturday. Seems an odd time for a wedding but—"

"Really?" Ellie exclaimed. "Are you sure?"

"Well, of course I'm sure, my dear. You hardly think I'd make a thing like that up? Here the doctor is now, why don't you ask him yourself?"

Ellie spun around to see Thomas emerging into the waiting room with his patient, issuing instructions on how the prescription should be taken. He looked up and caught her eye.

"Ellie!"

She didn't even need to ask. Thomas's expression was all the confirmation she needed. He couldn't contain his grin that was spreading across his face.

She ran across the little room and seized his hands in her own.

"Thomas!"

"I see you've heard then," he laughed, ducking his head shyly.

"Just now, from Miss Webb. So it's true?"

"Completely true. I would have told you myself, of course. We only agreed yesterday, but, well, you know what Endstone is like! I think half the village knew before I did!"

Ellie laughed, squeezing his hands tightly. His happiness seemed to be infectious; a broad smile was spreading across her own face.

"Oh, congratulations, Thomas. I'm so pleased for you. Really I am. For both of you."

"I'm a very lucky man, it's true. I can hardly believe she said yes."

"Of course she did, you goose! And she's very lucky too..."

"You will be there, won't you? You and your mother and Charlie? You're like my family here, it wouldn't feel right without you."

"Of course we will! We wouldn't miss it for anything!"

Fifteen

Ellie sat in the church between her mother and Charlie, perched on the edge of the pew. She was wearing the dress Mother had given her for her birthday, with a sprig of forget-me-nots at her breast, and more pinned to her broad-brimmed hat. The dress was a little warm for the weather, but it was the smartest thing she had.

In any case, for once she wasn't bothered by her dress, the uncomfortable pew, or the vicar's droning voice. All her attention was on the couple standing at the front, hands clasped, smiling into each other's faces.

Sarah's ivory-coloured dress was simple, but she looked beautiful as always. Thomas had combed his hair and – Ellie was amused to notice – there wasn't a single hole visible in any of his clothes.

The tiny church was packed; the whole village had turned out. It was strange to think that both Thomas and Sarah were relative newcomers to Endstone. Perhaps in another time they might have remained on the edge of things. But not now. Endstone considered them their own. Besides, Ellie wasn't the only one glad of something happy to celebrate.

At last Reverend Chester declared them man and wife. Camille handed her sister the bunch of wild flowers she had been holding, and they proceeded up the aisle, showered with flower petals by the congregation.

Everyone spilled out into the sunny square, laughing and talking and greeting each other. The reception was to be at The Dog and Duck and all the villagers had brought something to contribute. Ellie clutched her tray of sandwiches carefully, keeping an eye on Charlie as he toddled ahead, trying, as always, to keep up with the older boys.

As she followed his darting form, a half glimpse of another familiar figure caused her stomach to flip-flop. Ellie pressed her hand to it and scowled. "No!" she said.

"Eleanor?" Mother had appeared at her side and was looking at her in confusion. "Who are you talking to?"

154

"I don't know," Ellie answer truthfully, then, as Mother's frown deepened, added, "no one."

It wouldn't be him anyway, she told herself. He had been avoiding all gatherings for so long – why would he turn up for this one?

At the pub, the party atmosphere continued. In a strange way, it reminded Ellie of when war had first been declared. How excited everyone had been, she thought. How hopeful.

She was pleased to see that Mother was talking to some of the ladies from her WI group. It was not long ago that she would have stood haughtily on the edges of things, refusing to talk to anyone but her own family.

Ellie leaned against the outside wall of the pub, nibbling on a sandwich. She was joined there by Dr Mertens, overjoyed at his daughter's marriage. After they'd discussed Thomas and Sarah for a while, the doctor took Ellie by surprise with a change of subject.

"You know, Thomas and I are very grateful for all your help at the surgery." And as Ellie tried to brush this off, he continued, "No, really. I'm not sure what we would do without you. You are very good with the patients, Ellie. And very quick to learn when I show you something. Have you thought about what you might do in the future? In terms of work, I mean."

Ellie felt her eyebrows rise. No was the truthful answer. All her life, other people had talked about her future in terms of making a good marriage and being a good wife and mother, and nothing whatsoever to do with work. Ellie had imagined her future very differently. She wanted to get out of Endstone, to see the world, to be part of history and not always watching from the sidelines... But work had rarely entered into her thoughts. If she'd imagined it at all, she had supposed she might be a clerk, as Aunt Frances had been before the war.

But now, she *was* working. She'd even managed to do what she'd always imagined to be impossible; to get Mother's blessing for it. She couldn't decide if this meant she was closer or further away from her dreams than before – after all, it was hard to picture a future that didn't involve the war.

She realized she still hadn't answered Dr Mertens' question and looked up apologetically. He patted her on the back.

"It seems you have a lot to think about, Ellie," he

chuckled. "But make sure you do. And come and speak with me anytime you like."

"Thank you," Ellie said earnestly, "I will."

"And now I think I will go and replenish my plate. Can I fetch you anything?"

"Oh, no, thank you. I should go and make sure my brother has eaten something other than cake."

The doctor re-entered the pub and Ellie set off across the square in pursuit of Charlie. Her gaze was fixed so low that she didn't see Jack until she was almost on top of him.

They stared at each other in silence. His eyes ran over her dress, but still he said nothing.

"Nice to see you too, Ellie!" Anna declared, laughter in her voice. Ellie hadn't noticed her beside her brother.

"Oh, hello, Anna," Ellie said, collecting herself. "Hello, Jack."

"Are you impressed I managed to get him out here? It took a whole week of persuasion, I can tell you! I promised him cake. There is cake, isn't there?"

"Oh. Yes. Yes, there's lots of cake," Ellie said, trying to match Anna's breezy tones, but failing.

Anna looked back and forth between the two of them and then gave an exaggerated roll of her eyes.

"Right, well, as entertaining as this conversation is, I'm starving. I'm going to get some food. You look very pretty in that dress, by the way, Ellie. Doesn't she, Jack?"

She marched off without waiting for his reply.

Jack opened his mouth. Then he closed it again. "Me too," he blurted. "I mean, I'm going to get some food." And he bolted after his sister.

A growl emerged from Ellie's throat before she could stop it. "Oh, for goodness—"

"Lellie?" Charlie had appeared by her side, jam smeared over his mouth and hands, and even in his hair.

Ellie contemplated telling him off and frog-marching him to the fountain to scrub him clean, but instead she seized him in a crushing hug.

"I love you, you little vagabond."

"Lel*lie*," Charlie protested, squirming until she released him.

It was several hours later when they left the party. Mother had excused herself early on, but Charlie was having so much fun that Ellie was reluctant to drag him away. It was approaching bath time now, and most of the remaining revellers had been drinking beer for some time, and were beginning to get rowdy.

"Come on, jammy-chops. Home time."

Charlie put up a token fight, but Ellie could see him pawing sleepily at his eyes. They strolled hand in sticky hand back up the hill towards home.

The sun was low in the sky, making the light soft and yellowy. So Ellie wasn't sure at first that she could trust her eyes when she saw a figure leaning against their fence as they approached.

Charlie had no such doubts. "Jack!" he exclaimed, letting go of Ellie's hand and pelting towards him.

Humph, Ellie thought. *He needn't expect me to forgive him so quickly!*

"Hello, Charlie," Jack laughed softly, ruffling his hair. He looked up at her. "Hello, El."

Ellie could feel a ball of heat, starting at her collarbone, spread up towards her face. Charlie was burbling away happily but she cut across him. "I don't know what you're doing here, Jack Scott, but I do know that I have *nothing* to say to you!"

The words felt so final. She felt unwanted tears

spring to her eyes. She kept her chin raised and her gaze steady.

Jack dropped his head. "No, I know. But I have things I want to say to you, if you'll let me." He was rooting in his pocket. "Here, Charlie, mate. I made this for you." He produced a small wooden soldier and pressed it into Charlie's chubby fist.

Charlie laughed delightedly and ran for the front door, calling. "Mummyyyyy!"

Ellie felt a jolt of panic, and began to follow him.

"El—" Jack began again, grabbing her arm.

"No, Jack! A wooden soldier might be enough for Charlie, but it's not enough for me!"

"I know it's not. I just want to talk to you."

"Well, you can't! *I* can't! I have to . . . I have to give Charlie his bath."

She turned towards the front door, which Charlie had left wide open, and jumped when she saw Mother standing there, her mouth pinched.

There was a moment's silence, and then Mother said, "*I* will give Charlie his bath. I expect you back in *twenty* minutes, Eleanor." And with that she turned on her heel and closed the door behind her.

160

Ellie stared at it, feeling abandoned.

"Crikey, even your mam thinks you should hear me out." Jack gave a nervous grin, but Ellie simply glowered at him and stomped off back down the hill.

His long legs soon caught up with her, and they fell into stride. The silence stretched on until Ellie couldn't bear it. She spun to face him.

"*What*, Jack? *What is it?*"

He staggered to a halt. "I know, I'm sorry, I know," he exploded, tugging so hard on his hair, Ellie expected to see clumps come out in his hand. "I *know* ... I just ... I don't know where to start. I've left it so long—"

A spluttering sound escaped Ellie's lips and he looked at her with eyebrows raised.

"I *know*..." He sounded as though he were trying to soothe a skittish horse, or dog ... or himself. "Ellie, I've wanted to speak to you. Of course I have! You must know I have! But I haven't known where to start. I'm not the same person, El."

The sick feeling in her stomach was back. They walked on for a while in silence, reaching the edge of the square.

"I don't know if I'll ever be the same person again."
His voice was so quiet it took her a moment to be sure
he had really spoken. It was thick and low. His eyes
were on the ground. She took a step towards him.

"Jack..."

"I've missed you so much. Every day. But it's as
though ... as though... How can I speak to anyone?
You haven't seen it, El. You don't know..."

"So tell me!" she snapped. "You're my best friend! I
thought we shared everything! How can I know? How
can I possibly, possibly know, if you don't tell me?"

"I know, I know." His voice was barely more than a
low moan. She took another cautious step towards him,
reached out her hand, but didn't touch him. "El ... the
things I've seen. How can I ever be the same?"

She waited patiently, her hand still outstretched.

"Just before they found me ... before they realized.
There was this ... I don't know, battle, I suppose. This
man ... this *boy*, barely older than me he was, El.
Samuel he was called. Good bloke. He looked out for
me. Knew I was underage, and took care of me."

Dread pooled in her stomach. The sandwiches and
cakes had turned to lead.

"He was killed, El. Not just killed. Blown to pieces right in front of me. I *saw* the pieces." He looked up at her apologetically, but she motioned him on. "I mean, one minute he was a bloke I knew, a friend . . . the next, he was *pieces*.

"It was shortly after that they realized I was too young. And, God forgive me, El, I was delighted. I wanted nothing more than to get the hell out of there and come home. But I got here, and it was like home wasn't the same any more. How could I sit in my mam's kitchen drinking tea, and play with George, and fiddle, and cycle, and talk to you . . . when Samuel will never get to do any of those things again? And nor will any of those other blokes. Such good blokes, El. Just normal blokes. . ." Tears spilled down his freckled cheeks.

Ellie's hand, still outstretched, reached up to his face and wiped the tears away. Her other hand joined it and she took hold of his face. Her grip was strong. "Jack." She took a deep breath. "Jack, I'm so sorry."

He tried to move away, but she held him tight.

"I'm so sorry, but why didn't you *tell* me? I know I wasn't there. I know I can only imagine it. But you

163

could only imagine losing your father, and that didn't stop me from speaking to you about it."

"I know. . ."

"You're my *best friend*. This is . . . too much for you to be coping with alone," she said fiercely.

"You're right, El. You're right." He was sobbing now.

"El, Will saw it . . . saw Samuel too. He was sad, of course he was, but it was like it was nothing. . . He's seen a hundred more like that. It's like they stop meaning anything. . . You're just glad it's someone else, not you.

"And everything at home. . . I never want to go back there, El. Never! But everything here seems so pointless, so . . . *ridiculous*. A wedding! The factory . . . the shop! How can anyone care if they know what's going on out there?"

Ellie suspected that if they stopped caring about such things they would soon lose control of everything, but she also sensed that this was not what Jack needed to hear. She looked at her friend, his crumpled face still between her hands. Truth be told, she didn't know *what* to say to him. She could scarcely imagine what he had experienced.

164

She dropped her hands and looped them behind him. Then she stepped into his arms and wrapped her own around him tight. She squeezed as though she were lifting one of the filled shells, all her muscles straining against his tense form, until he relaxed against her. She could feel his hot tears spilling into her hair, his breath juddering against her. Still she held tight, as though he was drowning and it was only her keeping his face above water.

"I'm sorry, El..." he began a few times, but each time she shushed him. Eventually, his breath and heart began to steady.

"I've missed you, Jack," she ventured cautiously. "I've missed you so much. There have been so many things I've wanted to speak to you about..."

"I know," he said, his voice muffled as he spoke into the top of her head. "I want to hear it all... And there's so much I want talk to you about. My dad—"

Just then, Ellie felt something sail over her head, missing her by millimetres. She glanced up and saw Jack's brother, George, and Olivier Mertens, slingshots in hand, looking sheepish.

"Hello," Jack said, his wry tone almost as it might

have been a year ago. He stepped out of Ellie's arms, but kept one of his around her. "What's this, then?"

George was looking at his brother warily but seeing Ellie's reassuring smile he hazarded, "Well, that mushy stuff needed breaking up."

Jack dropped his arm and cast around for a missile of his own. The two younger boys ran squealing into the twilight.

"I should be getting home," Ellie said, feeling strangely shy. "Mother told me not to be long."

"I know," Jack agreed. "It's ... it's good to have you back, El." Before she had time to anticipate it, he swooped down and dropped a kiss on her cheek. Then he was gone, jogging after his brother, a clod of earth in his hand.

Ellie stood and watched him until he was out of sight.

Sixteen

Ellie stumbled out of the factory alongside Daisy, happy to get out into the daylight and fresh air.

"That Mr Jenkins is something else, isn't he?" Daisy huffed as they marched briskly in the direction of the train station. "He's more of a whiner than my little sister."

"'*Ladies*,'" Ellie impersonated, in a high-pitched, nasal tone. "'Please can we *try* to keep chatter down to a minimum? We *all* have work to do here...'" Jack was the real expert at mimicry, but her attempt was still enough to render Daisy incoherent with laughter for a few moments.

"'And, Mrs Lenehan, if you could *please* cover your shoulders, I know it's hot, but we *must* maintain

167

decorum,'" Daisy snorted, before collapsing into such hysterical giggles that she couldn't continue. She groped around in her pockets before sobering up abruptly. "Oh, rats!"

"What's wrong?"

"I've left my handkerchief!"

"Again?" Ellie laughed.

"I know, I know. I'll have to go back and fetch it."

"No, come on, you can get it tomorrow. You'll miss the train if you go back now."

"I know, but it's the third I've left this week. Mam will have my guts for garters if I go home without another one."

Ellie protested, but Daisy was immovable.

"No, it's all right, honestly. You go on. But it's more than my life is worth to go back without it again."

The girls waved goodbye to each other and Daisy trotted back in the direction of the factory.

The train was waiting at the platform and Ellie clambered aboard, wondering whether Mother would have left something for her tea, and what she should make if not. Already her eyelids were heavy, her body readying itself for its nap.

There was a sudden flash of light and the train rocked. *Lightning?* Ellie's weary mind had barely formed the thought just as the flash was followed by a great roar of sound. Suddenly she found herself on her knees on the floor of the carriage. A glance around confirmed that the other passengers were on their knees too.

The sky flickered again, the train shook, and once more it was followed by a terrifying growl. Shouts and screams arose from the other passengers.

"Bomb?"

Ellie wasn't sure she'd said it aloud, but next to her a man had staggered to his feet and was looking out of the window.

"No, it's the factory," he said. He offered her a hand and pulled her up next to him.

Through the window, Ellie could see smoke billowing from the factory. Bursts of flame appearing through the bulging, black clouds, followed always by cracking thunderclaps. And – was she imagining it – could she really feel the heat from here?

"Oh, my God."

The passengers poured back on to the platform.

Ellie followed them, her limbs moving mechanically, like a sleepwalker, her mind hazy.

Finally, a clear thought dropped into the middle of it, like a pebble into a pond.

Daisy!

She began to move slowly in the direction of the factory, gradually gathering speed. She felt hands grasping at her, was dimly aware of cries of "Where are you going?" and "Don't be daft, lass". But she could see others, their faces panicked or strangely blank, moving in the same direction.

Soon they were running towards the smoke, towards the terrible sounds. Ellie felt her breath come in jagged gasps, felt her heart begin to beat an erratic, almost painful drum.

More pebbles were dropping into the pond, faster and faster, the waters becoming more agitated.

Daisy... The other girls – they had been so quick out of the door after their shift had finished, but lots of the other women had been slowly gathering their things, laughing and joking or grumbling together...

The shells. All those shells. All that ammunition. They were always so careful; nothing that could cause a flame was allowed anywhere near the factory. What could have set it all off?

And ... *Jack*. Was he working today? He'd been doing so many extra shifts, but she couldn't remember...

She was running full pelt. Her eyes were streaming with the smoke; she began to splutter and cough. All around she could hear awful moans and screams.

She was close now. But how could she get closer? All the buildings adjacent to the factory were on fire too. Explosions were still going off, making her jump with every boom and crash. The heat was incredible. Sweat was pouring down her face and back, and the smoke was so thick, it was hard to see anything. Occasionally, a figure would stagger out of the darkness. The voices emerging from all around were eerie; wails of pain and terror, cries for help and names shouted in panic.

"Milly! Milly!"

"Help me, God help me!"

Another pebble dropped into the now churning waters... Was this what it was like on the French fields after a battle?

Ellie ducked lower, where the smoke was less thick, and stumbled forwards. The gap between explosions seemed to be growing.

And suddenly, still in the distance but getting closer, she could hear bells clanging – ambulances and fire trucks arriving from Canterbury. How had they got here so fast? Or was it longer since the first explosions than she realized? All sense of time was lost in this nightmarish landscape.

As the fire trucks arrived, the shouts increased. Individual sounds were harder to make out now; it was all one great cacophony. Men and women were stomping through the darkness. The hoses had been turned on the flames and gradually they began to die down.

Daisy, she thought again. She realized she'd been hoping to see her in-between the station and the factory, but the other girl must have been faster than she'd thought.

Oh God, what if she was inside? Could anyone have survived?

"Ellie!"

She spun round. Peering through stinging eyes, she

saw them – the women from her shift. Ida and Helen and Martha and Sally . . . and Daisy!

Ellie rushed towards her. Daisy was sitting on the ground, her face and hands and clothes filthy with smoke. She was shaking and crying, but as Ellie ran her eyes quickly over her, she could see no visible injury.

"You're all right, Daisy. It's all right." She pulled her friend in close, pressing her head against her chest. "Sssh," she soothed as Daisy sobbed against her.

Looking over Daisy's head, she saw Mr Jenkins lying nearby. He too was smoke blackened, and coughing as though he might choke. Leaving Daisy with the other women, Ellie ran to him. The ambulance workers were moving through the crowd now, carrying stretchers and hastening to the most urgent-looking cases. Ellie dodged between them.

"Mr Jenkins! It's Ellie Phillips." He wheezed and coughed some more. "Here, try to sit up a bit; it will make it easier to breathe." Bracing her arms underneath his torso, Ellie levered him up to a sitting position. Seeing a nurse busy nearby, she ran and took one of her canteens of water, which she held to his lips, encouraging him to take little sips.

After a few moments, he was breathing more easily, and Ellie sat back on her haunches, still resting her hand against his back.

An awful scream, penetrating through all the other sounds, made her look up.

Jack!

There he was, staggering through the debris with a woman's form draped in his arms. The screaming was emerging from behind the woman's hands, which were covering her face. It was unlike anything Ellie had heard before. Jack lowered her to a stretcher beside the nurse, who immediately turned her attention to the casualty. Ellie saw Jack's hands go to his thigh.

As he began to stumble away, Ellie staggered to her feet. Quickly she led a nearby ambulance worker to Mr Jenkins, then she ran after Jack. She caught up with him just as he sank to the ground, still clutching his right leg, which stuck out awkwardly from his body.

"Jack!"

"Ellie?"

His face was slick with sweat, causing black rivers to trickle down it. She dropped to the ground next to him and gently lifted his hands. Blood poured from a

174

ragged mess on his leg. He groaned. Ellie swallowed, her tongue thick in her mouth. Taking the end of her skirt in her hands, she tore of a wide strip from the bottom, and tied it tightly around the wound.

"I know, I know, I'm sorry," she said in response to Jack's jolting gasp. "We need to try to slow the bleeding until a doctor can see you." She kept her hand firm against his leg, despite his moans of pain. "You're going to be all right, Jack," she said, forcing her voice to be calm and steady. "You're going to be just fine."

Jack's gaze has been unfocused, but now it latched upon her. "Don't leave me, El. Please don't leave me."

"Of course I won't leave you!" she said with a smile. "Where would I go? I'm going to get you some water. I'll be no distance," she went on as he began to protest. "You'll be able to see me the whole time. Keep your hand tight against your leg – here." She replaced her hands with his own and ran to fetch another canteen of water.

With a lurch of her stomach, she saw that her hands were wet with blood. But the water was too precious to use for washing them. Returning to Jack's side, she held the canteen to his mouth so that he could drink.

"Not too fast. Sip it."

She tore a new strip from her skirt and replaced the old one. She was pleased to see that the blood was slowing now. An ambulance worker hurried up to them.

"He's bleeding a lot from his leg," Ellie told him. "I think ... I think there might be something in there."

Jack groaned again.

"All right, there are more ambulances on the way. We'll get him on a stretcher and on to an ambulance as quickly as we can. Are you all right to wait with him until then? Do you need any medical attention yourself?"

"I'm fine," Ellie said briskly. "We're fine."

As the man walked on to the next crowd of people, Ellie fixed her eyes on Jack. "I'm not going anywhere until you're safely in an ambulance, all right?" she repeated.

Jack nodded. His hands were clamped on top of hers over the wound. He laced his fingers between hers. She saw another black trickle roll from his eye, down towards his chin.

She leaned forward and kissed it away, the taste of

176

salt and ash on her lips. She kissed the top of his head and the space between his eyebrows. Then she rested her forehead against his, their eyes close together as if she were transmitting directly into his brain the thought that he would be fine, that she wouldn't let anything happen to him.

And suddenly their lips met.

All she would remember afterwards was the noise all around them; the smell of gunpowder and smoke and blood; the feeling of their hands pressed so tightly together she no longer knew whose fingers were whose; and his lips, so strangely soft, at once familiar and alien, against her own.

Seventeen

On her way to visit Jack, Ellie called into the village shop. Of course, she knew that anything he really needed, his mother and sister would already have taken to him. But Mabel had been loath to leave his side and Anna had been tending the shop on her own. She doubted his sister had had time to think of bringing him treats.

A newspaper, she thought. Jack had been complaining of being bored, cooped up in the house. A bit of news from the outside world might help with that.

She pushed the door open and greeted Anna. Sure enough, she was alone behind the counter.

"How's the patient today?" she asked.

"He was still asleep when I left this morning. You

probably have a better idea than I do, you've been round to see him so often," Anna returned. She gave a sly smile, but behind it she seemed distracted, anxious.

Ellie laughed, a little awkwardly. As she moved over to the rack of newspapers, she could hear its echo clanging around the shop.

She drew the top newspaper towards her, quickly scanning beneath the headline that had snared her attention:

GREAT BRITISH OFFENSIVE
ATTACK ON 20 MILE FRONT IN THE SOMME
MANY PRISONERS TAKEN

She skimmed onwards. The article focused on the gains made by the Allies, but slipped in amongst the rhetoric were horrifying hints at the loss of life on both sides.

"Isn't it terrible!"

Dr Mertens' voice behind her made her jump. Camille and Olivier were beside him, their faces equally grim. "Just terrible. They're not putting this in the papers, but I think the casualties will be like nothing we have seen before. I don't mind admitting, Ellie, I am glad to be far away from it all, with my family safe in England." He tousled Olivier's hair.

Ellie nodded, thinking guiltily of how glad she was that Jack was home too – injured, but far away from the battlefields. She glanced over at Anna, who was facing away from them, stacking shelves. This explained her distraction, she thought sadly. They must all be so worried about Will.

Deciding against the newspaper, Ellie instead bought a bag of sugared almonds. She said goodbye to Anna and the Mertens, and continued on her way.

So many people must be waiting anxiously for news of their loved ones, she mused. Her thoughts wandered to her latest letter from Aunt Frances. Her aunt had written of the hundreds of people lining the railings outside the hospital in Brighton where she worked, hoping to see their loved ones as they arrived from France, or simply showing their support to the returned heroes.

So much waiting and watching.

But wasn't for her. She wanted to do something. She wanted to do *more*.

Arriving at the Scotts', Ellie knocked, and on getting

no response, let herself in.

There was no sign of anyone in the kitchen, so she headed up the narrow staircase to the tiny room Jack shared with George. Here she found both boys; Jack propped up in his bed, George bounding around telling him enthusiastically about a football victory against some of the boys from a neighbouring street.

Jack was smiling, but looked exhausted. George broke off his story to greet Ellie, but then looked all set to resume.

"Georgie, mate, don't take this the wrong way, but I really don't think there's enough room in here for the three of us. Why don't you go downstairs and make some tea?"

George pulled a face. "*More* tea?" he protested. "You haven't even finished your last cup!"

"Well, why don't you go and see if Doc Thomas and Sarah are on their way? Mam said they were going to visit."

"All right," George agreed cheerfully, before clattering out of the room and down the stairs.

Ellie and Jack laughed, and she perched on the end of his bed, presenting him with the almonds.

After asking Jack how he was – much better, just desperately bored – Ellie remarked, "Your mother isn't here."

"No," Jack replied, his face falling. "Oh, El. Something terrible has happened."

She frowned. *Now what?*

"It's my dad. He's ... he's been arrested."

"Jack! No! Whatever for?"

He scowled, the cold look flickering back through his eyes. "It's so awful. I'm ashamed to say..."

She waited patiently, lowering a hand to the bed beside his.

"They think ... they think he might be responsible for the explosion."

"What?" she whispered, her throat dry.

"It seems ... he was sent home about an hour before it happened. He was caught stumbling around, reeking of booze. I didn't know anything about it at the time – I was working in a different area. He's been getting worse and worse, especially since he realized they were going to start calling up married men to the army. Now that I've been out there, I can understand anyone not wanting to go, but..."

Ellie bit her lip. Jack's mother had told her something of his father's reasons for being so against war, but had sworn her to secrecy. It felt wrong to keep a secret this big from Jack; her silence felt as much a betrayal as a lie would have been.

"I'm amazed he hadn't been fired," Jack went on, sparing Ellie a response. "Anyway, it seems he must have ignored the order, because he was found passed out when the ambulance workers were going round. Still stinking of beer, of course. It doesn't look good, El. All that damage; those people who died; all those injured. They'll be looking for someone to blame. No one will ever forgive him if he caused it. I don't think *I* could; I'd be so ashamed." His voice was sad rather than angry.

Ellie took his hand and they both fell silent.

"There are so many things that could have caused it," Ellie said at last. "Think about it: the place was like a giant box of fire-crackers. In a way, it's a wonder something hadn't happened sooner."

"Yes, but, El—"

"I know, I know. But, look, we don't know anything yet. So far all your father has done is be in the wrong place at the wrong time. I know it's hard, but there's no point in worrying about it until we know more, so try not to. You've got to concentrate on getting better so we can get you out of this room before you go completely mad!"

He smiled at her and squeezed her hand.

Just then they heard the front door and George's energetic tones.

"Sounds as though Thomas and Sarah are being treated to the match report," Jack remarked with a wry grin.

Soon the room was packed and this time Jack was firm in dispatching a grumbling George to make tea.

After everyone was settled in the small space, Thomas asked Jack about the injury.

"Looking all right, I think. I tell you, I started feeling better as soon as they got that chunk of shell out of me at the hospital!" he boomed. Ellie smiled to hear him more like his old self. "Anyway, Mam changed the dressing again earlier and it was looking much cleaner."

"Good, good. No signs of infection?" Thomas asked.

Jack shook his head.

"You did well, Ellie," Thomas said, turning to her.

184

"All that training with Dr Mertens has clearly paid off."

"It wasn't much," Ellie said. "There wasn't a lot I *could* do. I couldn't even clean the wound."

"No, but like a true medical professional, you dealt with the most urgent need, namely staunching the flow of blood. You know, she might well have saved your life, Jack."

"She's been doing *that* my whole life," he replied with a grin.

"I'm sure the training with my father helped," Sarah said, in her soft voice, "but he insists that Ellie is a natural."

Ellie blushed, but Sarah was not to be deterred. "It's true; he speaks about it all the time. It's your instincts, he says."

"Just like your father, Ellie," Thomas said proudly.

Ellie hesitated. A little seed of an idea had been nestling in her brain of late, sending out tiny shoots until it was anchored and strong. Suddenly she found she wanted to share it.

"I have been thinking," she began, "that maybe I should be doing more..." She looked around at the circle of supportive faces, but in the end it was Jack's she focused on. "I have been thinking that maybe I could train ... as Aunt Frances has done ... that maybe I could be a nurse."

All three of them were beaming at her. It was as though she had got a question right at school. For a moment no one said anything, but then Jack laughed.

"That's our El. For all the time she spends with her head in the clouds, she doesn't half take a long time to see what's in front of her nose."

Ellie gave him a shove. "What do you mean?" she demanded.

When he'd finished grimacing and groaning in mock pain, he chuckled again. "I think you might be the very last person to come up with that idea, Ellie Phillips."

Now they were all laughing. Ellie raised her hand to shove him again, then lowered it pensively.

"I can think of one person who certainly won't have had that idea, and will be none too pleased to hear about it."

Jack and Thomas nodded seriously. Only Sarah looked confused.

"Who's that?" she said, looking at Thomas.

But it was Ellie who replied: "My mother."